# TRAMP
## STEAMING

www.BarbarianSpy.com

BarbarianSpy
Toronto
Australia

# TRAMP
# STEAMING

## habu

# CONTENTS

# CHAPTER ONE: ETIENNE

Taking him. All of him inside me. Fucking me doggy style on a platform bed in a seedy beach hotel cabana room just steps away from the ocean north of Suva, in Fiji, across a thin line of coconut palms from the top of the beach. He was a muscular hunk, atypically younger than I was by a year or two, crouched over and mounted on my hips, his strong hands grasping my wrists, my hands buried in the mattress to hold me steady. Atypically because I was used to going with older men. His teeth chewing on my earlobe while he pounded, pounded, pounded away inside me.

He released one of my wrists, rummaged around in the drawer to the nightstand without missing a beat of the fuck, came out with what I took to be a small bottle of poppers, and ran it under my nose. Whatever it was, it didn't enhance anything sexually. What it did rather than the expected was that it put my lights out just after he went rigid, jerked, and gave me his load.

When I came to, I was stretched out, flat on my stomach, appendages all akimbo. Through the open sliding glass doors out onto the beach, the sun was going down. Another spectacular sunset over the South Pacific Ocean.

Etienne—if that's what his name really was; he had been quite secretive about letting me see his passport when we'd entered Fiji—was gone. And the cabana had a deserted feeling about it. The eerie quiet prompted me to drag out of the bed, staggering a bit and shaking my head to try to shake off what had to be more than just the one bottle of scotch we'd polished off together earlier in the afternoon, and to check out my valuables. My former valuables, I must say. Etienne had cleaned me out. At least he'd been gentleman enough to leave me my passport and my clothes—other than that Western-style leather-fringed vest he'd admired so much when we first met in Nouméa, on Loyalty Island in New Caldonia. And my fancy tooled cowboy boots. He'd wanted them too, I could tell.

I was a pushover for French men. And Etienne had been more exotic than that. Some Maori or other native South Pacific Islander breed in him. It gave him bulk and the look of carrying that bulk well—of being overpowering. He certainly overpowered me— emotionally as well as physically. I was on a discovery tour of the South Pacific in the summer of my junior year at Princeton. Not so summer down here in the islands, but still warm enough for the beach life. I was looking for life experiences. I was getting them.

I'd done Sydney and had enjoyed the laid-back gay scene there—and fully intended to go back there before going home to the States. And then to Auckland, in New Zealand. I wanted to work on my French and was told I really should take a swing through the South Pacific islands, so I decided to do so. I had the means and the time.

I picked up Etienne—or, rather, he picked me up—at a hotel beach bar in Nouméa, New Caldonia, during a night of beach dancing—me just in a Speedo, my cowboy boots, and the fringed Western vest. I found myself dancing with a real hunk of a man—a ruggedly handsome hunk of muscle who spoke French, looked at one with the islands, had a great smile, and was wearing a skimpy bathing suit with an intriguing zipper down the pouch that I could tell was barely containing a monster cock and balls, and swaying oh-so flexibly and provocatively in front of me. He spun away long enough for me to regret his absence and then was back.

In the interim I had visions of opening that zipper in the pouch of his swimsuit to examine the jewels tucked inside.

"Nice vest and boots," he said when he had swirled back to facing me. He said it in English, obviously already fingering me as American, but with a heavy French accent.

He spun away again to be replaced by someone not half as alluring—leaving me to wonder if he'd done that on purpose—and giving me that image of his zippered pouch again. The "someone" touched me intimately as we were dancing, obviously wanting a hookup, but he paled in comparison with the guy with the French accent. Then that guy was back, flashing a toothy smile, moving close into me.

"You have a beautiful body," he whispered in my ear as he leaned into me. "I want to fuck you. Do you take cock? I see that you keep eyeing my zipper. Want to blow me?"

I'd had far too many beers to be coy and the night was moving on—and I'd come to the South Pacific to get laid, so I told him yes—to both a blow job and a fuck.

"Now?" he asked, putting his hands on my hips and running his fingers on either side under the waistband of the Speedo.

"Now is fine," I answered.

"You have somewhere we can go, or do you want to entertain this crowd?"

In short order we were in my hotel room, with me kneeling before him, slowly opening the zipper on his crotch pouch, finding the jewels as glittery as I had imagined, and taking that monster in my mouth. It was a surprise—browner than the rest of his tanned body, almost black. Long and thick. And he wanted it deep-throated. I did what I could.

He fucked me up against the wall, my legs hooked on his hips, one of his strong hands holding my wrists captive together above my head, pressed to the wall. He fucked me doggy style as we slithered over toward the bed. He fucked me missionary style on the bed. We slept the few hours before dawn, and then he fucked me on the bed with him lying on his back, trapping my arms and legs with his and fucking up into me as I yodeled to the ceiling.

He ordered room service for breakfast, told me if I really wanted to polish my French, Fiji was the place to do that. Then, using one of my credit cards, he booked sea passage and a hotel room for both of us in what he said was a special sort of beach hotel in Suva, in Fiji.

"We're going by tramp steamer to Suva," he said. "It should take three days. I think you'll find it interesting. Slow and easy." And it *had* been an interesting experience, with Etienne fucking me slow and easy the entire three days in a small cabin on a working island supply ship on a bunk meant for one. I'd come to Nouméa by tramp steamer from Sydney, so I'd known more-or-less what to expect. I'd expected boredom, but on the sail from Sydney to Nouméa I hadn't had Etienne.

After making the reservations, Etienne pulled me into his lap, facing him, as he sat in a straight chair by the breakfast table and pulled me on and off his cock to what was my fifth ejaculation and his third in the little time I'd known him.

And here, a week later, in Fiji, I'd endured two more deep-throated blow jobs, he'd fucked me three more times, and then he'd rendered me unconscious and practically wiped me out of all my liquid financial assets, my credit cards—and my beloved fringed vest and fancy tooled cowboy boots.

No sense in fighting it now—there's no way I could regret his servicing of me or the pride I'd acquired of being able to deep-throat a monster cock. He was, I was sure, half way back to New Caldonia now to fleece his next tourist.

# CHAPTER TWO:
# CHRISTOPHE

I pulled a pair of low-rise shorts and a sports shirt out of the closet, put them on, leaving the sports shirt open and not tucked into the shorts, and padded down to the hotel reception desk to start the process of reporting I'd been ripped off, was temporarily destitute, and needed help to start the process of canceling cards and replenishing my funds. I was barefoot. I did have tennis shoes and a pair of boat shoes still, but I was in mourning for the beloved cowboy boots and interested in evoking sympathy at the desk by pointing to where the cowboy boots no longer were on my feet.

As I was talking with the hotel assistant manager, who was all sympathy and clucks, covering, no doubt a few snickers concerning the circumstances of my plight, probably having this problem regularly and even, perhaps being in on the take, I noticed another hotel guest, who was sitting in the lobby and reading a paper, starting to show interest.

The man possibly was in his early forties. Very well put together, dark complexioned and with dark curly hair. He was slim but well muscled and, like me, was wearing shorts and an open sports shirt. Unlike me, he had open-toed sandals on, but no socks. He had that artist aspect about him and was unmistakably French. He was, in fact, much of what I had thought I'd meet and have experience with in the South Pacific. A mature French artist type with a mature model's face and aspect and a sensuous smile. Visions of Maugham and Gauguin floated through my mind.

He also reminded me that I usually went with older men and that my atypical tryst with a younger man hadn't gone too well.

He was turning that smile on me now, as he stood, gave enough pause for us both to know he was commanding my attention, turned the smile even more sensuous, licked his lips, puckered them a bit, and blew a bit of a kiss. Only the French would do it this way, I thought. But the French could get away with it.

I followed him into the hotel bar, where he was already perched on a stool and turned toward me. The barman was at hand, ready to take the Frenchman's order. I recognized the barman who seemed to be on much too large a scale to be standing behind a hotel bar. He had been a performer at the beach party the previous evening. He looked at least half civilized today, although I could see that the tattooing over half his face was real—that it hadn't been makeup the previous night when, as a fully tattooed Samoan warrior, he'd performed a dance in just a loin cloth at the beginning of the festivities on the beach—a loincloth that had disappeared later in the evening to a general gasp of awe.

"Would you like a drink?" the man perched on the barstool asked me. His voice was a smooth baritone. He exuded self-confidence. He was as French as French could be. Both of us knew that, if he wanted to fuck me, he would. This was a gay resort. That's what guys came here for.

"Can't afford it at the moment, although I certainly feel like I need one. You probably heard back there in the lobby that I've been wiped out and am not fluid at the moment. I doubt I have enough cash for the next few days to stay in my hotel room, let alone to pay for drinks."

The man shrugged. "I'm sure I can help you with both the drinks and hotel room—mine."

"In exchange for what?" I asked, knowing what, but curious what he'd say. He obviously had heard that it was another man, staying with me, who had robbed me.

"I'm sure you know what in exchange for," he said, showing me a nice smile. "That Etienne you spoke of at the desk is somewhat of a legend around here, although the hotel staff won't admit it, for financial reasons of their own. And I'm quite aware of what he does with young men like you. I assure you that I'm very good with the cock too. And you are a sweet young piece. I'm very happy to help you out in your time of plight for cocking privileges. American, are you?"

"Yes, I'm American," I answered.

"Nice. Some of my most memorable fucks have been of Americans. They are so naïve of the possible positions, but oh so willing—and appreciative."

"You don't believe in foreplay, do you?" I asked.

"Not when we both know you want me to fuck you. You'd want me to fuck you even if you weren't in trouble."

Thus it was I met Christophe Fortier.

\* \* \* \*

"Let's go over to a table overlooking the beach," the man said, "and I'll treat you to a bit of foreplay. I know Americans like that. Then we'll fuck. I'll try you out to see if it's worth my while to help you."

He was holding both drinks he'd ordered—mai tais. Not my drink, but he was paying for them. He also was controlling them. I followed him to the table, where he sat in a chair parallel to the view and waved me to one facing the beach. I was surprised we didn't just go to his room, but he didn't seem all that anxious to proceed, even though I could see from the skimpy material of his shorts that he was hard.

"My name is Christophe. Christophe Fortier. The name is French, of course. Comes from 'stronghold.' That's me—a regular fortress. And you, you're American. You look a bit young to be traveling in the South Pacific alone. Let me see your passport, please."

I showed it to me, knowing he wanted to make sure I was old enough to fuck. I was both amused and flattered. The age of consent here was sixteen, I'd been told. I had no illusions that much of my success in attracting men was that I looked considerable younger than I was.

"I wasn't alone, of course," I said with a smile. "But I would have been better to have been alone."

"No, but you picked up Etienne in the islands, didn't you? You didn't bring him from New York or Miami."

"No, I came from between those two—Philadelphia. And without Etienne. I'm a student—at Princeton, New Jersey. Oh, sorry, my name is Nathan Cassatt."

"Ah, railroads."

I was somewhat taken aback. It was a Mainline Philadelphia name, yes, but for a Frenchman in the remote South Pacific to know about the Pennsylvania Railroad was really something. Not having everyone around me know was one reason I've come this far for my junior trip. It made me wonder if Etienne had known too and had been more attracted by the money than by my body.

"Yes," I answered. "But I came this far to escape that—and to improve my French, if you must know."

"Would you prefer we spoke in French?"

"I'd like to try that," I said. "If I have trouble, your English seems superb and we can always revert."

He'd finished his mai tai and signaled for another—for both of us, although mine was only half gone. He moved into a smooth French, which I found so much more sensuous than English. He also laid his hand on my thigh. I wondered why we didn't just get on with it. I thought he was wrong about Americans wanting a lot of foreplay. I reacted better to someone who approached me and said he wanted to bang me—and then did, wham bang. Of course, that had been Etienne's approach.

"I'm surprised you know the name and the connection to Philadelphia," I said in what seemed to be halting French against his fluid diction in both languages.

"I lived and worked in New York for several years—honing my skills and looking for publishers. The Cassatts do some publishing, don't they?"

"Yes," I answered. But I was a bit nonplussed by that question. They didn't do publishing all that openly. A small, niche publisher, headed now by my father's boyfriend, James, using my father's money and name. The same boyfriend who had taken my virginity and initiated me into wanting sex from men.

"I know of that because I am a writer," he said. He opened the briefcase that had been at his side, hanging from a strap on his shoulder, when we'd come to the table and that he'd put on the floor beside his chair. I could see that he had a laptop computer in there. He took it out; placed it on the table, the screen in front of me; and opened it to a file.

"And you write about the South Pacific?"

"I write about young men being fucked by other men in the South Pacific. Look out toward the beach, Nathan. What do you see?"

"Beach, ocean, palm trees . . . bathers."

"Men bathers, Nathan. Randy men, all working on making or being made. This is a gay beach resort. Men come here to fuck. You came here to fuck. I came here to write stories about men fucking. Men fucking men." He moved the laptop closer to me.

I would have looked at the file on the computer screen if I hadn't been shocked by what he said next and latched my gaze on his face.

"Tell me, this Etienne, was his cock thick and long? Did you have any trouble taking him? Did he do more? Did he fist fuck you?"

"Excuse me?" I said. But he had his hand on my cock through the material of my shorts. He knew that my cock had lurched at that question.

"Was he horse hung? I see that you're approaching that yourself. A bit of a surprise for someone on the small and slender side as you are. Has anyone told you that you are more beautiful than handsome? A beautiful blond. Do you do modeling in the States? Or perhaps pornographic films? Is that James Miester, who runs the Cassatt publishing house, into more than pornographic publishing?"

"That's a lot of questions," I said. "But, yes, Etienne was horse hung"—I'd rendered "horse hung" in English, as I couldn't quite manage the French pronunciation Fortier had given the term. "No, I didn't have trouble taking him. I know I look young, but I'm experienced—and have been reamed wide before Etienne. I came to the South Pacific just for such a stretch. I'm sorry, did I word that wrong? I don't know the French word for 'reamed.'" I could be as straightforward as he was being.

"No, I think you worded that perfectly," Fortier said, with a small laugh. "You probably wonder why I asked. There, read the story I wrote last night—there, read it on the screen."

I began to read, and my jaw almost dropped to my chest. He had written about me and Etienne—at the dance on the beach. I could tell it was us, but it was written even more sensually than the actual experience. I found myself trembling. The actual events had been arousing, but this story made them even more so. I looked up at him.

"This. This is Etienne and me last night. You obviously were observing us. Is this what you write?"

"Yes, this is what I do. I travel regions of the world and write collections of short stories. I am doing this in the South Pacific now."

"You mean like James Michener and *Tales of the South Pacific*? He's already done that."

"Yes, and made a lot of money from it and from the musical made based on it. But mine are different. Mine are in French, for specific collectors who pay a lot of money for them, and mine are hard-core male pornography. And . . ."

"And what?" I asked. It came out a little breathlessly as he was gripping my cock hard, and I was hard for him. If this was foreplay, he was still taking the direct route.

"And my stories are based on observation and experience. That is where men like you and Etienne come in. That is why I might be offering you support until you can regain your finances. I know now, knowing the family you come from, that you will regain your finances. But in the days before you can do that . . . this isn't Philadelphia or New York. I know that eventually you'll be set up again—through contact with an American Express office, and there are a few scattered around on the South Pacific Islands. But—"

"You said you *might* be offering support. You already offered it before."

"I must be sure. For me to support you—I'm not made of money as you are—I must have compensation.

19

Inspiration for my stories. Observed experience. Do you understand?"

"I'm not sure."

"Observed experience may not be accurate. I write from observation, yes. But I write more from my own experience. What I have done myself—what I have done to young men like you. What I have men I bring in to do to young men like you—that I observe and usually participate in. It's why I asked you if you could take an extra-large cock—and maybe two at once. Do you understand what I'm telling you? I write for a highly sophisticated, demanding, and searching audience. I don't write vanilla stories. Have you ever had two men working you over at once—hard?"

I didn't know what to say, so I just shrugged.

"How far into the story have you read on the computer screen? Did you read of the sex on the beach?"

"No. I've read of how provocative and sensual you made the dancing at the beach party."

"Read on," he directed. As I turned my face to the computer screen, I heard and felt the unzipping of my shorts. He gripped my cock, skin on skin, and started a slow stroke as I read. I looked around, in shock, afraid that we were being observed. But this was a gay resort. I'd seen men fucking in the lobby and no one had intervened.

In the story, a complete departure from what really happened, Etienne was coaxing me out onto the beach, beyond the fringe of the lighting from the beach party, where the moon shining off the lapping waves on the beach provided the light.

"This isn't as it happened," I muttered.

"You went to your hotel room," Fortier whispered. "The story had to extend from what I observed. I had to capture where it might go. That's why you're reading this. I need to know how authentic it is—how natural the progression is. Location isn't all that important, although the readers will be more aroused by a beach at night than a hotel room. It's one reason why I asked you about the size of Etienne's equipment and how easily you took it. Why I asked about Etienne's fetish. You didn't have time to find out Etienne's fetish? I have to know if my development beyond my ability to directly observe was authentic. And I have to know if you would go where the Etienne of the story took you."

I moaned as I read on in the story—not just because of what was written, but also because Fortier was slowly jacking me off. Embarrassed, I took another quick look around. The bar was deserted at this time of day other than by the native islander barman. He had come out to the side of the bar, leaning against it, watching us, his dick out and in his hand. His cock was as oversized—a real tropical sea slug—as the rest of him was.

There would be no objection or interference from that quarter. In fact, looking over at the door in the lobby, I saw that the barman had closed that. Probably locked it too. Of course, anyone could appear from the beach, but no one did. From here I could see that the beach was nearly deserted. This obviously was a gay hotel. Most of the men who had been there when we sat down had made their hookups. This activity went in cycles. Regardless, those left were interested in each other, not in what was happening in this bar.

Even if any of the male hotel guests came in from the beach, they were likely to do what the barman was doing—watch the show that Fortier was putting on, using me. He had one hand on my cock under the table top and the other gripping the back of my neck and messaging it. His face was pulled in close over the top of the laptop, watching my expressions as I read his graphic story.

"Are you writing a story about this, what you are doing to me here, in your mind even now?" I asked in a whisper.

"Of course I am. Later I'll have to fill in the emotions it's bringing out of you—or you will, if I let you stay with me. Now read the rest of the story on the screen."

In the story, I was on my back on the sand and Etienne was stretched out beside me, rolled toward me. We already were naked, and he was holding me in a close embrace. He was giving me a hand job, preventing all attempts of mine to work him as well. He wanted me milked first and said so.

"Have you read where he jacked you off first?" Fortier whispered.

"Yes, but that wasn't what he did. He worked me with his mouth first—at great length."

"Because I was right? Because he is magnificently hung and wanted you able to take him? Because he wanted to do more—wanted you more open?"

"Yes. That's what he said. That's what he did."

I read on, my trembling increasing, my moans deeper and prolonged—and not just from the effect of Fortier's hand job in the present. It was the attention Etienne gave me in the story, on the beach. So much different, so much more than he gave me before he fucked me in our room last night. But somehow . . . somehow so Etienne.

In the story he worked me hard, but it was with his fingers, at first, and then his fingers up to his knuckles, and finally his whole fist. Fisting my hole, stretching my channel. My right leg was raised up his beefy chest, the ankle hooked on his shoulder. My left leg bent, my buttocks rolled up to give his fist fullest access. He was deep kissing me on the mouth, sucking on my tongue, pressuring it with his teeth—bringing me to the edge of fearing he'd bite it off. Just like, now that I thought about it, what he'd done at the height of passion last night. And he had his fist up my hole. Holding me tight, preventing me from writhing beyond limited bounds, my huffing and deep moaning competing with the sound of the surf.

My explosion in the story was gigantic, my cum arcing up high toward the sea in multiple spouts. Only then, me exhausted and trembling from the fist slowly moving inside me, did the Etienne of the story turn me on to my knees and forearms and fuck me like a dog to his own ejaculation.

"Oh, god, Oh shit, I'm gonna come," I muttered in the real time of the bar as Etienne creamed my insides in the story. And then I did, my wad hitting the underside of the table and dropping back onto my thighs.

Christophe laughed. "Now you know why I get paid good money for my stories."

My eyes darted over to the bar, where the barman was arcing his cum on a tabletop too, and then going around behind the bar for a rag to clean off the table and going back to nonchalantly polishing glasses.

"It wasn't like that. He didn't . . ."

"He didn't fist fuck you to an ejaculation?" Fortier asked, pulling back from me, but leaving me sprawled in my chair, my dick hanging out of my shorts. He hadn't freed his, although I could see that he was hard inside those shorts and was leaving a precum wet spot.

"But was that a natural progression of what he would do with you?"

"Yes, I guess so." And I did guess so, it seemed, even at the time, that Etienne was headed toward something I'd never done before—almost welcomed him doing.

"And would you have let him fist fuck you?" Fortier asked.

"Yes, I guess," I responded after a bit of silence. If I could take it, I thought, although I didn't say that.

"Have you been fist fucked before?"

"No . . . I haven't." There was just enough pause before I completed the denial to tune Fortier into there being more—something I wasn't saying. And there *was* more. There was James' fetish. The anal balls.

"You hesitate. There's been something comparable?"

"One sex partner of mine," I murmured—I was not about to reveal who it was though—"One sex partner liked to use a string of graduated anal balls."

"Graduated? Graduated to what diameter?"

"Uh, I can't remember . . . but yes, I can. He was proud that he'd found them. The largest three inches, I think."

Fortier whistled. "That large? Why that's probably the diameter of the heel of my hand. You've already been there in reality—or nearly there." He raised his hand for me to see and turned it slowly in the air, bunching his fingers together, exhibiting it for me at all angles. He gave a little laugh and I shuddered. "Would you say the heel of my hand was three inches across? Maybe. Maybe a bit larger, though. Etienne's a much bigger man than me. What would you say his dimension would be? Four, five inches? And I understand it was his fetish. That if he'd been with you longer . . ."

I shuddered again, looked away. Fortier gave another low laugh. "I didn't write anything that Etienne didn't have in mind for you until his greed interrupted the progression of his seduction. You are so expressive, you know." Christophe continued. "I think we're going to write great stories together. You both fear and are drawn to what I am suggesting, aren't you?"

"Yes," I answered in a small voice.

"Good. Remember all of your emotions—both now and when . . ." He let that just sink in, which it did—it sank right into my gut.

I needed to change the subject. "You had something else so right in the story—well a couple of things. That his cock was darker than the rest of him, and that he liked to give the impression he'd bite my tongue off."

"Ah, yes. Well, you aren't the first young man Etienne has brought to this hotel. I have other stories in the collection, taken from first-hand accounts. Other young men spoke of Etienne fist fucking them. Others have said he used the tongue technique so that fear would heighten their arousal. That's why I included those elements in my story. But you say he didn't get as far with you as the fist fuck."

"No, no he didn't."

"Is that a tone of regret I hear from you?" He was still holding his hand in the air, the fingers bunched, revolving the hand so that I could see it from all angles.

I didn't answer him. I just shrugged. But in my mind, I was lying on the bed on my back, Etienne hovering over me, latching his eyes on mine, gauging my reactions as he worked his fist up into my ass. Trembling at the image of that, I was melting to the possibility of it—the need for it. I had come to the South Seas for experience in the kinky and bizarre—and challenging.

"So, where does that leave us?" I asked "Do we go to your room now?"

We both knew what I was agreeing to.

"Yes, but still as a trial. I needed to hear you say that you would have let Etienne fist fuck you. My stories are about taxing sex. If you come to my room, you will have to let me take you places sexually you probably never have been before. You will have to pay your way by informing my stories. But, then, you say you have come to the South Pacific to deepen your experience. I will do that for you. Just imagining the fist fuck made you come big. I think you want the experience. Do you wish to come to my room now—knowing what I'm going to do to you?"

"Yes." Why the hell not. He was right. I didn't come on this journey for vanilla experiences.

* * * *

26

It took him a long time to get to it. If I'd known it would be as taxing as it was, I'd probably have tried to beg off or ask him for even more preparation.

He started off vanilla—except for the dildo part—with me bent over the bed and him kneeling behind me. Him even more appealing naked, in full up-curved erection, than clothed, pulling my cock and balls between my thighs and giving them and my hole almost endless attention. Slathering me with lube. He said I'd want to be as open as possible, and he was doing everything he could to make that happen. When he had three or four fingers inside me, I asked him if he was doing it now—fist fucking me. He just laughed and said, "Nowhere near. You'll know it when it's happening."

I was also fooled by the dildo, thinking he was fucking me with his cock. But I'd seen his cock. He had it out and was hard. Long but not particularly thick. *This* was thick. I nearly fainted when he took the dildo out and put it in front of my face where I was pressed, cheek to mattress, to the bed. The dildo was as thick as his wrist.

"I've taken that?" I whispered, in wonder. "I can take your fist?"

"Look at my hand, Nathan," he said. The hand was long and slender, but I could readily see that it was wider where it attached at the wrist—wider even than the dildo. I moaned at the thought of where we'd be going from here.

But we didn't go there immediately. "Time for a break," he said as he moved away from me and came around to the side of the bed. He came down onto the bed, adjusting pillows behind him to sort of recline up against the headboard, grabbed a pack of cigarettes from on top the nightstand, and lit up.

I rose up from my bent position over the foot of the bed and stretched my muscles. I felt as open in my channel as I'd ever felt. "A break?" I asked.

"For me, not you," Fortier said. "Ride my cock. I want to see if you're any good at it."

I climbed up on the bed, threw my leg over his pelvis, and lowered myself on his staff as he held it erect with one hand, still using the other to smoke his cigarette. I rode the cock from every conceivable angle for a half hour or more with the goal of making him put that cigarette out and become lost in me. I eventually succeeded, with him alternating from grabbing my hips and arching his back as he grunted and groaned and pulled me on and off his cock to my lying flat on my back with his ankles crossed on my chest, with me slamming my buttocks hard on and off his cock and him stroking my cock to an ejaculation that barely preceded his.

He arched his back and moaned, an arm thrown over his face, as I felt him flow two and then three times in the bulb of the condom deep inside me. Then, suddenly, he was animated, jack-knifing himself from under me, jumping off the bed, pulling me back into the bent belly position over the foot of the bed, and I screamed out in surprise and pain as he rammed the thick dildo back inside me and pistoned it hard and deep.

I writhed under him, begging for mercy, but answering each declaration from him that I could and would take it with a "Fuck yes. Fuck me, fuck me, fuck me." My eyes opened wide in another scream when I felt his own cock entering me on top of the dildo.

"Shit. God, I don't think I can take this?" I cried out.

"You can take it. Your passage is fine with it," he growled in my ear. "You were prepared well for this before. And you'll be taking more than this soon."

Soon came almost too soon for me.

I was spread-eagled on the bed, restraints running from my wrists to each end of the headboard and on my ankles to the ends of the footboard. The roping attached to my ankles was loose, allowing me to bend my knees and spread my thighs. Pillows were under my buttocks, raising my hole to point at the edge of the ceiling across the room. A ball gag was jammed in my mouth.

"You'll be glad for the gag and the restraints," he told me. And he was right, as I tried screaming and writhing free as he gave me the experience of fist fucking—probably not nearly as much as one trained to it over time, but enough to have almost made me black out.

He was wearing tight rubber gloves, and he kept slathering his hands and my passage in a white grease as he moved from hand to hand, pushing them inside me with his fingers bunched, slowly opening me to the hands, as I strained at the restraints, bit into the soft rubber of the gag, rolled my eyes wildly, and huffed and puffed at the exertion required to take him.

He informed me when a fist was inside me, up to the wrist.

"There, it's in," he whispered as he leaned close over to me. His other hand had lost the glove and he was stroking my hair and kissing me on the cheek. "I want you to remember all of the sensations of this," he murmured. "That's why we're doing this. I want you to have experienced it and to be able to describe it to me—both the physical and emotional sensations—in detail. I'm going to make you come with the fist now."

And he did. He moved the fist inside me, a knuckle of the hand rubbing my prostate, and in short order I exploded and fell back on the bed, exhausted, almost ready to black out—with one last arching of the back and scream as he extracted the fist. He leaned over my body, tearing the gag out of my mouth, possessing my mouth with his, jerking at his cock, and spouting great gobs of cum out over my belly.

Emotions? He wanted emotions and physical reactions? Well, for that latter, pain, of course, and the feeling of being impossibly stretched and possessed. The need to shit but not being able to, but also the feeling that my prostate was being pushed up into my sac as a third ball—throbbing and aching and feeling the buildup of the cum—the feeling that I was about to explode, wanted to explode, and that, in doing so, I'd be torn apart. And still wanting it. The emotion of wanting it, despite the pain, of wanting to be fully possessed. The helplessness of being restrained. Not only of being fully controlled and filled but then, also, the glorious feeling of being able to do it—to take it. And when the explosion of the release came, a high like none other. Wanting the high again, as crazy as it sounded.

So, did I want it again? No, of course not . . . but maybe—maybe yes, if I could get that high, could have that feeling of having taken it. Already wondering about a bigger hand, an invasion further up the arm. I'd seen up to the elbow in vids. Could I?

I lay there, on my back, the restraints removed, still moaning, my legs still bent, spread apart, my insides feeling hollow, like air was rushing up my passage, toward my stomach. I let out a mighty fart, and Frontier laughed and moved from the bed over to the table where his laptop was open.

"I don't know if you noticed that the story based on you and Etienne was written with you as the narrator—first person in the character standing for you. I want to read to you the passage of the fisting on the beach. And I want you to give me the emotions that go with that—taken from what we've just done. I want the story to read like it really happened—from your perspective."

I lay there, feeding him what underlay what he'd already written, and when I was able to rise from the bed, he beckoned me to come over and read it. I saw that he had added the perspective of Etienne as well—the feel of having his entire hand inside me, of working the prostate, of the high arousal it brought him, and the prodigious release. He had made the story come alive. I had never read anything as taboo and pornographic and, at the same time, as arousing and as movingly described. He had told me that these were specialty stories, sold to a select few at high prices, and I now could see why they went for high prices.

Now, I was surprised to realize, I nearly ached to do it again.

But we didn't do it again. Later that night, he took me into a new story, a different one, but one that was served by the fisting—the coaxing of my channel impossibly open.

We were on the bed—only returning there after a long recovery period of polishing the story and eating a meal in the hotel restaurant—and returning to the bar for a nightcap. The same bartender was there, although there was another one on duty as well. The big bartender kept looking at me, undressing me with his eyes. He made me shudder. I'd rarely seen a man as big as he was—and as primeval, with that tattooing that accorded him such menace when he performed his Samoan warrior dance for the tourists—making it provocative in keeping with this hotel being a gay resort.

When he took me to bed, Fortier instructed, "Awareness. Remember everything again. You have a talent for it. Not just for the sex but for the description of the physical feelings and emotions you receive from the sex. We will write excellent stories, you and I."

It was the first inkling that I had satisfied him and that he would continue to support me until I could regain my financial footing.

I didn't know, though, what special story he could get out of the fucking we were doing. He called it the position of the crab. He was on his back on the bed, and I was draped over him, looking up at the ceiling, my legs bent and my hands stiff-armed into the mattress on either side of his chest, while he fucked up into me from below. Him being long and me still being very open, there was no trouble with him maintaining purchase inside me, and I held steady, on top of him but suspended over his torso, and he thrust up inside me, with his hands gripping my waist.

I understood what was new—what was fodder for a story—though, when I heard the door of the room open, and saw the bartender—the massive Samoan warrior dancer—from the hotel bar move toward us. He was naked and in angry, magnificent erection. Fortier was scooting our bodies down toward the foot of the bed as the Samoan advanced. When the Samoan grabbed my ankles and wishboned my legs, causing my body to drop fully onto Fortier's torso and Fortier's cock to slam up deeper inside me, I knew what the next story was about.

I cried out in both pain and ecstasy as the Samoan drove his cock inside me above Fortier's already-buried cock and started to piston me hard.

Then, for the first time, I understood what he'd meant when he asked me if two men had ever worked me hard together. And I fully appreciated the preparation Fortier had gone through and the experience of having been fist fucked earlier in the day. I never before would have thought I could take a double, and if I'd gotten into the situation, I probably would have tightened up enough for there to be nothing but pain if two men insisted.

But now—oh, shit, that Samoan; thick, long, fucking deep, hard, that tattooed, fierce face pushed into mine, while, underneath me, Fortier held steady and hard, also deep inside me even if not as thick as the Samoan, eventually also counterpistoning with the Samoan and taking me to paradise—now I thoroughly enjoyed the fuck two men could give me together.

\* \* \* \*

"See anything you like?"

Christophe had caught me eyeing the men on the beach at the gay hotel in Suva. The beach had been made private here and was well screened at either end—although I occasionally could see motorboats drifting in toward the beach, carrying men with binoculars. Those on the beach all were men, many in couples or more, and in various stages of dress and undress—and undressing each other. Sucking each other. Fucking each other—right there on the beach.

There were more older men on the beach, though—prowling about—than there were younger ones. Mostly the younger ones were posing and the older ones were shopping.

Fortier and I were sitting in chairs at the top fringe of the beach, in the shadow of palm trees, both in Speedos. Fortier was pounding away at his laptop, presumably writing up a story to go with last night's threesome between him, the Samoan bartender, and me—with me in the middle. I was daydreaming and sitting sprawled in the chair and working on recovering from what the Frenchman had put me through the previous day.

I also, admittedly, was watching the other men on the beach and, yes, gauging them in terms of arousal. There were quite a few who did arouse. Some of the older men were well preserved but there, also, unabashed were ugly men, and fat men—undoubtedly rich men. Most of the latter were watching the eye candy and working on adding to the arousing men's bank accounts. I marveled at how many of the young studs were willing to go into the bushes with old, fat men. I was sure it was for the money and mentioned that to Christophe.

"Some of those old, fat men are horse hung or have very soft mouths and great technique," he said, without looking up from the computer. "It's darker in the bushes Many a young man is more interested in the size of the cock inside him than the weight of the man fucking or sucking him. If you are interested in testing that out, I know of a couple of men out there on the beach who can make you forget they are ugly and fat. In fact, it would make for a good story because many of the men who pay dearly from my stories are ugly and fat."

I turned my eyes back toward the beach. More than a couple of the older men had passed close to us as well and given me the eye. As if on cue, one of them pulled down the front of his suit and flashed me what must have been an eleven-inch cock. And true to what Christophe had said, my own cock lurched in answering arousal. It seemed quite evident to these lurkers and shoppers, though, that I was with Christophe—and that Christophe could meet my needs.

He certainly had done that and more so far.

"Those men might have been good looking when they were young," Christophe said, again with his head buried in the computer, making me wonder how he'd seen the old geezer flash me, "And most assuredly they had the eleven-inch cock then that they still have now. But, to their credit, they are more likely to know how to fuck you to heaven now than they did when they were younger and way less experienced. But you want to take them young, I'm sure. Hard body is a thing with you, I've observed."

"There are some good-looking younger men out on the beach, yes," I answered.

"Any you want to fuck?"

"What do you have planned now, Christophe? Have you finished a draft of the story from last night? Can I look at it yet?"

"The research isn't finished yet. I need you to select a couple of muscle men off the beach. Hard bodied, as I know you like them. Hard bodied like Etienne was. See anything you like?"

Just then I saw a young blond guy, walking along the surf line all by himself. He wasn't what Christophe was asking me to pick out, but, for some reason, he arrested my attention—and he aroused me in a way I'd never been aroused before. I'd always looked at men as possessing me—James had trained me to that early. But this man . . . he brought out different sensations in me. Strangely enough, I envisioned him as under me, with my cock inside him.

He wasn't a muscle man. He was slender—well muscled enough—but not bulked up, and he walked with the grace of a dancer. He was nude, carrying a Speedo dangling from his hand. There was nothing oversized about him—he was a bit undersized in the classic "David" look—but that only enhanced the boyish innocent aura he exuded. He was beautiful and seemed shy, walking with an introspection as if he was the only one on the beach. There was a sadness about him, and I had the sudden strange urge to go to him and embrace him. And to . . . I couldn't even think about it; it wasn't my role in the world of men with men.

There were, of course, men pacing with him, working on making their moves. All kinds of men—all being drawn to him. If he noticed, he didn't indicate that he did. I had the sensation of vultures circling him, poised to swoop on him all at once—and to tear him apart with their teeth.

He hadn't gone too far down the beach than he met the old man who had flashed me walking toward him from the other end of the beach. The old man flashed the young blond with that big snake of a cock of his, and, just like that, the young blond separated from the rest of the vultures and followed the old man into the bushes.

"Those two, perhaps?" Christophe asked.

My attention was switched to two muscle men—one in his late twenties, perhaps, and the other in his early thirties—coming out of the surf, arm in arm. Both were hunks, naturally. I would not expect Christophe to draw my attention to anyone who wasn't. I couldn't quite tell their nationality—Spanish or Brazilian maybe. One thing that distinguished them, though, was that they seemed to have their eyes fixed on me as they walked out of the surf and to a couple of large, colorful towels stretched out on the beach not far between the surf line and were Christophe and I sat. Rather than settling on the towels, they remained, drying themselves off with other towels, but half turned toward us, their eyes fixed on me, whispering to each other. I had the sensation that they were posing for me.

Now that I thought about it, I'd seen them standing out in the water earlier with another young man. The two seem to have been working the young man together. Christophe had drawn my attention to them at the time, but there had been so much to see that I hadn't watched them for long.

"Yes, they're very nice," I answered.

That seemed to be enough for Christophe. He rose from his chair and moved down the beach to meet the two where they stood over their towels stretched out on the sand. The three conversed for a few minutes, doing more looking at me than at each other. They walked to me together.

"Go with these men, Nathan," Christophe said. "Let them do anything they want with you."

They both fucked me on their towels, one after the other, but both being involved at all times—one at my tail, in doggy or missionary style, and the other at my head, feeding me with his cock. By the time they were sharing me, both standing, facing each other, with me flopping around between them, being double played like a calliope, we had gathered a crowd, standing around and watching us and pulling at their own dicks—giving the same circling vultures aura that I'd seen when the young blond was walking the beach. Christophe sat off to the side, stroking the keys on his laptop.

The story he let me read later had both forms of the double penetration in it that I had experienced that afternoon and the previous night. But the scene he set was of me walking along the surf line—just like the young blond I'd seen and been aroused by and snatched off the beach and out to sea by a couple of beefy men in a canoe (both of whom seemed to sound an awful lot like the Samoan bartender), where my character is taken to a much smaller island, hung by his bound wrists from a tree limb, and double assaulted six ways from Sunday by those two and other men doing some sort of victory celebration on the island.

The plotline seemed outlandish to me, but Christophe made it arousing with what always was his elegant and detailed writing. That evening we sat over the laptop, while he scoured my brain for the emotions and physical feelings of being doubled and polished up his story.

We did that, I'll say, until there was a knock on the door, and Christophe opened it to let in a large-boned, ruddy-looking man who must have been a Swede or a Norwegian and at least fifty years old—gaunt and weather-beaten.

"This is Captain Thorensen, Nathan. He's going to spend a few hours with you."

What Thorensen wanted to do was to fist fuck me and then just to fuck me silly on the bed missionary style with his big bone. He also wanted to nearly choke me to death, being interested in edging and breath play while he was fucking me. Several times I nearly blacked out while he was fucking me and stroking my cock with one beefy, gnarled hand and choking my throat until my eyes bugged out with the other.

When he was done with me—Christophe having just looked on, pecking away at his laptop, as I almost died—and he was leaving, the gaunt man from the north turned to Christophe and said, "He'll do. We sail at 4:00 p.m. tomorrow."

When he was gone and when I could manage to at least barely croak, I asked the questions that were burning in my mind almost as hotly as my throat was burning. "What did he mean by I would do? What's he the captain of, and what's this about sailing at four tomorrow?"

"He's captain of the *Pitcairn*, one of the supply tramp steamers plying between the islands. We're booked to sail as passengers on the *Pitcairn* tomorrow bound for Tahiti in French Polynesia. I need new locales for the anthology I'm writing, and I wouldn't want you to miss out on seeing Tahiti on your grand tour of the South Pacific."

"And it hadn't occurred to ask me if I wanted to go to Tahiti? I need to get my finances reestablished."

"Why should I give a shit what *you* want?" Christophe responded. "Until you are hooked up again, you are dependent on me. And you needn't try to tell me that what you're getting isn't exactly what you were looking for in coming to the South Seas. They have an American Express office in Papeete. You'll be reestablished when we get there, you will have had your adventure, and I will have an anthology I can sell."

I opened my mouth to object to something—but I couldn't think of anything to object to. He was right. Even in suffering the breath play, I was gathering sexual experiences that I'd always wondered about. Who would have known that I could take fisting so casually, for instance—or doubling, for that matter.

And I wanted to know the story Christophe would make out of tonight. I wanted to read his arousing take on it. I wanted to be part of telling his readers what it was like to experience that. He had won me over to this storytelling program. I wanted to know what was next.

But there was another question. I repeated it. "What did the captain mean by I would do?"

"You were our entrée on board. He had to approve of you. Obviously he does. We'll be at sea for a couple of weeks from here—on an isolated sea, a ship full of randy men and no exit—a ship where the captain's word is law. I am thinking of the short stories I can write. You can think of the adventure."

And, strangely enough, the way he put it in his rich French baritone—the way he had with words and with manipulating me—all I did see was the sensual adventure on the offing.

\* \* \* \*

"This isn't . . . this is snuff," I said, with surprise. "I'm sure he never meant to go that far."

We were huddled around the laptop in the hotel room that evening. Christophe had spent longer than using tapping out a story. His concentration had been total and his brow knitted. His hand had also been busy working his cock whenever he took his hands off the keyboard to concentrate on the word he wanted to write or image he wanted to create. He had me quite curious. He hadn't focused as fully on the writing in the previous stories he'd written from the experiences he developed for me.

In this story he had me picked up in a bar on the waterfront, taken in a backroom by a hulky sailor, and choked to death during sex. The sex scene was quite graphic and long. My character in the story suffered— tried to resist and get away but couldn't manage it. Still, he had come in great gobs before he expired. It was clearly drawn that he had been sexually aroused by his own death. I had never read anything so pruriently brutal.

If it hadn't made me so hard and dripping as I read it, I would have taken my eyes away from it in disgust.

The strange thing was that I easily could marry up what Fortier had written with the sensations I had while the tramp steamer captain was choking and fucking me. I wouldn't have any trouble at all providing the emotional underpinnings for this story. I just didn't know whether something like this should be available to read at all. I had to think about that. I hadn't thought of questioning anything of his I'd read earlier.

"Yes. I watched you when Thorensen was choking you while he was fucking you. At any moment he could have gone over the line and snuffed you."

"And you would have let him?"

"Of course not."

"You would have stopped him in time from where you were sitting across the room and watching? I've never seen a story that went all the way like this. Have you written this sort of stuff before?"

"Snuff stories? Yes, of course. I get more money for these from my select clients than for most of the others. Having a gang of thugs beat a young man to death while passing his ass around for all to enjoy is more brutal than this—and it sells the best."

"And you specialize in these?"

"You should read the vampire collections I've written. I'm particularly fond of one titled *Vampire LaCour's Second Coming.* My protagonist fucks his victims to death as he sucks their blood, both fluids needed to bring him back to a high-toned body, and his victims die with a smile. Perhaps after we do the South Pacific, you might like to return to Europe with me and meet my model for the vampire. He's very much into the role. He would enjoy you. He has a magnificent cock."

"And the men you mated him with . . . who he . . . ?"

"They all completed their roles with a smile on their faces."

The look on my face made him laugh. "No, of course he didn't really kill them. But, yes, he did suck some of their blood and fill their passages to the brim with his cum." He laughed. "And, no, I didn't hear of any of them turning into vampires from the experience."

Christophe had risen from the table where we'd both been looking into the laptop monitor, had gone to a bureau and rummaged around in a drawer, and came back to me. He had the dog collar around my neck and pulled tight, almost choking me, before I knew what he was up to. A leash was attached to the collar, and he almost pulled me out of the chair with a jerk.

"Over to the bed. Now. More research."

The wrist restraints were still in place at the corners of the headboard from the previous day of the fisting scene, and Fortier manhandled me into these. In short order he had me on my knees on the bed, my arms incapacitated, and was mounting me from behind. One of his hands was under my belly and the other held the leash tightly, arching my head back.

He took me swiftly, coordinating the jerk of the leash—and the sensation of choking by me—with thrusts of his cock and release of the tension with withdrawal.

He was barebacking me, not having taken the time for a condom—or for lube for that matter. I still was dilated well from his fisting and that of Captain Thorensen, whose hand was significantly bigger than Christophe's was. So, I could take him.

43

But the fuck was raw, brutal, and choking—and in some primeval way, I was fully into it—slapping my buttocks back into his thrusts, the thrusts compensating for the jerk of the collar on my neck.

With a little cry, Christophe creamed my insides, pulled out of me, and pushed me over on my side, releasing the collar leash. He reached up and freed my wrists. My hands went straight to the collar, which I unbuckled and tossed to the side. Pulling myself up on my elbow and hanging my head down, I panted, fighting for more breath.

"I had to capture what the captain would have felt," he said. "Do you think you can put those two experiences together to help polish up this story I've written," he said. He was calm and matter-of-fact, as if he hadn't, only minutes before, been choking and fucking me to within an inch of my life.

"Yes, I said," with a gasp and a raspy voice. "I could have done that before you fucked me just now."

"But I fucked you good, didn't I? Made the emotions of being choked nearly to death fresh, didn't I?"

"Yes," I answered, still rubbing my throat.

"Yes to which question?"

"Yes to both," I answered—honestly.

"So, get out of the fuckin' bed and come over here and help me finish off this story."

That night he held me close and made long, slow, deep, languid, sex with me. We apparently were now beyond the condom stage. He hadn't used one for the choking sex. I'd thought it had just been an oversight when, in fact, it was a turning point in our relations.

"Live on the edge; live dangerously. I do," Christophe said. "It takes you higher."

Feeling his cum gush deep inside me and his cock churning around in his cum certainly did that for me.

The next morning, he pulled me over to the laptop, backtracked on his stories—made them ones of barebacking—and pumped me for details on how it felt, what emotions it pulled out of me. It aroused us both—I was feeling exceedingly sexy this morning anyway and had a perpetual hard on—and the session wound up with me sitting on his cock in his chair, facing him, in his lap, pumping myself on his hard staff in another bareback fuck. And then, quite soon, another.

Christophe must have taken something before we'd come to the computer. After that first ejaculation, he remained hard and took over pulling me on and off his cock, as I lay back in his grip, allowing my head to reach for the floor, my arms to dangle out on the carpet. He fired off again and again, causing his cum to flow around his churning cock and dribble down my thighs, taking me higher and higher to my own explosions— actual fireworks shooting up into the heavens in my vision. I felt so high that I thought maybe he'd slipped something into my morning coffee too.

I rose up and clung to him when his cock went flaccid at last and pulled his face into my chest, where he feasted on my nubs, causing me to ache to go again. We rocked back and forth, both panting heavily, both moaning low and sighing. He went hard again and gave me a weak ejaculation, which, nonetheless, was the sweetest of all.

"Remember this," he murmured. "Later, on the ship, we'll write a story of a young man being drugged and ravished again and again. Perhaps in an encounter in the same waterfront bar as the last story. Of course it will have to be placed before the other one. You die in the choking story. That one will have to be the last in the collection, I suppose. But now we must pack up and get to the ship."

"It's not leaving until 4:00 this afternoon, I thought."

"You will have duties in preparing the ship for sailing," Christophe said. "Serving the ship's needs go with the price of passage."

# CHAPTER THREE: AUSTIN

So this was what serving the ship's needs was about, I thought. I was riding the tramp steamer captain's cock in his cabin on the *Pitcairn*. He was on his back, and I was saddled on his hips and both rising and falling and rotating on the shaft, driven deep, in every direction imaginable. He had my full attention—and had had it ever since he slapped me around when I came to his room and was forced into giving him a brutal, face-pumping, deep-throating blow job. He then had demanded that I ride him well or he'd beat me—and I had every reason to believe him. In any event, riding him hard this way was giving me as much pleasure as it was him, I thought.

He was into what apparently was his fetish—chocking me during the fuck. He had his big, calloused hands wrapped around my throat, using them to pull me up and down on his cock. I, of course, was doing all I could to anticipate when he pulled me up by rising on my knees with his jerk to take the pressure off my neck.

Before I'd come with him to his cabin after dinner on the *Pitcairn* when it already was well out to sea, Christophe had taken me out on the deck and to the side of the ship. With a sweep of his arm, he'd taken in the expanse of the wide, empty sea, no sign of land or of another ship evident.

"I want you to think of this when you are with Captain Thorensen," Christophe said. "We are all alone—isolated—out here on the ocean. Here the captain of a ship is the law, a god unto himself. While he's fucking you, I want you to be aware that he can take anything he wants from you. He can beat you; he can choke you; he can fist fuck you. You already know he will do this."

I shuddered at the thought of this, more than half of which was arousal.

Christophe continued. "He can fuck you to death if he wishes, toss your body over the side of the ship, and that will be that. I want you to be thinking of how close you are to the edge of life and of the power he has over you. And then, if you are alive tomorrow, we'll put that into a story."

"But he can't kill me in the story, right?" I asked, trying to make a joke of it—a weak joke, to be sure. "I mean you already have a snuff story for your collection. I can't die twice in it."

"There are other collections I can put it in," he said, pulling away from the rail and walking away a few steps before turning and addressing me again. "I assure you that there is little limit to what I can do to you in a story—and not much in real life, either. And let's be honest, it's that edge you came to the South Seas to ride."

Shuddering again, I turned to see where he was going to find that the captain was standing in the hatch door Christophe was headed to. As Christophe passed Thorensen, I heard him say, "Rough him up as you like; he wants it rough."

I didn't remember having said anything of the sort, but here I was, out on the wide, empty sea, as Christophe had said, and there Captain Thorensen was, smiling a little smile and beckoning me to come to him. I did, but as I reached him, his smile morphed into a sneer, he backhanded me hard across my cheek, and I went down on the deck. He simply reached down, hauled me up with his strong arms, slung me over his shoulder, and carried me to his cabin.

He was too strong for me to resist him even if I saw any good that would do. I was exhausted from the other "serving of the ship" I'd done that day.

We had arrived at shipside shortly after lunch, maybe around 1:30 p.m. The crew was still loading the ship with supplies going to smaller islands to the east of Fiji. I was later told that supplies would also be taken on, first in Pago Pago, in American Samoa, and then again, after islands in the Cook Islands had been supplied, in Tahiti, before the ship swung north and came back toward Australia by way of the Line Islands, Kiribati, Tuvalu, and Solomon Islands.

"They're not ready to cast off yet," I said. "We're early."

"We're not early," Christophe responded. "Part of our passage is covered by you helping with the crew's tasks. I suggest you strip down to your shorts—it's going to get very hot working out here—and start lending a hand. Besides, they will all want to be able to inspect what the captain has bought for them. I'll go check out the cabins and start working on the 'drugged fuck' story."

"The cabins?" I asked. "We're in separate cabins?"

"Yes. I don't want my sleep interrupted."

It was only the following night that I understood what he meant by that. The first night, I wasn't going to get to my assigned cabin. I'd be in Captain Thorensen's bed.

For the rest of that first afternoon, I worked alongside the crew of the *Pitcairn*, hauling supplies on board and stacking them "just so" in the hold.

The crew of the *Pitcairn* was a motley collection and included one surprise. They were made up of various nationalities and colors and ranged from their twenties into their late fifties. There were two things that all but one of them had in common, though. They were body, if not face, beautiful—muscular and cut, little fat on any of them, the result no doubt of the physical demands made on a tramp steamer sailor. The other common denominator is that, throughout the afternoon, they looked at me with slitted eyes and great interest and showed every sign of maintaining hard ons.

The one exception was the surprise—and he stood out in such contrast that I had difficulty figuring out what he was doing on this crew. It was the young blond man who had walked by Christophe and me along the surf line at the gay resort hotel in Suva the previous day and who had let himself be lured into the bush by an old man with an oversized cock. He was working alongside the rest of us, although neither he nor I were able to hoist what the others did. He wasn't built for the work and he wasn't built like the others. It wasn't that he didn't have good muscle tone. It was that he was willowy and moved like a dancer. There was a natural sensuality and rhythm of movement about him, something slightly androgynous. Something that brought out my arousal in a different way than the men I wanted to fuck me did.

Throughout the afternoon, he stayed close to me. I got the impression he wanted to speak to me, but there were too many others around—too many giving me the eye. Giving him the eye too. I returned his gazes of interest with ones of my own, but I made no attempt to converse with him then. We would be on the sea for weeks. There was always time for that—and time for me to work out why he worked my emotions like no other man did.

Inexplicably, when I watched him, it was I who went hard.

The sailor who showed me where my cabin was later in the afternoon when the ship was under way and pulling away from the harbor at Suva, was all hands—touching me here and there, walking close behind me as he guided me through the narrow corridors of the ship. With a hand on my buttocks he turned me through a doorway and into a tiny room—more like a closet. But there was a bed and built-in cabinets on one wall and a door into what was the smallest head I'd ever seen—only room for a stool toilet and a tiny basin. The cubicle served as a shower too, with a shower head on the wall opposite the toilet and a drain in the floor in front of the toilet.

It was the bed that intrigued me. A single tray bed with high sides all around, The slats rising a good ten inches higher than the top of the mattress. I looked at the sailor, a question on my face.

"For rough seas," he answered. "So you won't fall out onto the deck and break your cute little neck."

"But the holes in its sides?" They were running down both sides and were stacked on top of each other, three to a row. The raised sides looked like Swiss cheese.

"To help the flow of air," the sailor said.

But the next night—not this night—I found out that the holes weren't for the flow of air at all.

And this night my ass was the captain's.

After riding his cock in a chokehold, I lay, splayed on the bed, panting and rubbing my bruised throat, while Thorensen sprawled his massive, Scandinavian frame on a chair across his commodious, well-appointed cabin, swigged beer, ogled me with a lustful stare, and reloaded.

"God, you're a sweet piece," he muttered. "Well worth the price. And if I hadn't been shown your passport, I would never have guessed at your age."

I was dozing when I heard the snap of the rubber gloves on his hands. I looked over to where he was standing next to the table where he'd arranged his empty beer bottles. There was a can of white grease on the table and black rubber gloves on his hands. I moaned at the realization of what came next. But there wasn't anything I could do about it.

He fist fucked me bent over the bed, my wrists tied together, arms stretched uselessly over my head, and my legs spread as wide as I could to accommodate as best I could the slow invasion of my channel with his greased fists, one after the other.

When he was done and we both were cleaned up, he took me to his bed, enfolded my body in his arms, and slept the night through with deep breathing and a slight snore.

He took me in a side-splitting fuck in the morning and then he sent me back to Christophe, who, sitting in a deck chair under cover on the port side of the ship, was polishing up a story on a young captive being fucked to death by a pirate captain in his cabin after a sea battle and sinking of the captive's ship. I arrived in time, hobbling and lurching against corridor walls—not all caused by the rolling of the ship—in time to add color to the story.

\* \* \* \*

"Do you mind if I join you?"

The young blond guy I'd dreamed about half the night while Captain Thorensen was fucking me looked up and gave me a look of noncomprehension. I immediately was crushed—rejected before I'd even had a chance.

But, no. He explained his response by telling me in hopelessly broken French that he didn't speak the language. He hadn't understood what I'd asked.

"How about English, then," I asked. "I was asking if I could join you." I had seen that he'd taken his lunch out of the communal mess hall and toward the bow of the ship, where he'd settled on a thick rope coil and turned his face from the ship's superstructure toward the direction in which we were steaming—east, toward Pago Pago in American Samoa.

That did the trick.

"Yes, English is good. And, yes, please do join me. I've been hoping to be able to talk with you."

Nothing like I'd been hoping for it, I thought, as I settled, cross-legged, on the deck beside the coil, facing north, looking at him in profile and being as surprisingly sexually aroused in looking at him from that perspective as from any other.

"Your English is excellent—an American accent. Are you—?"

"I'm from New Jersey. Toms River," the young blond answered. "I've escaped from NYU for a semester. Your accent is American too, isn't it?"

"I'm from Philadelphia. On my junior summer escape from Princeton." Princeton was a hop, skip, and a jump from either Toms River or New York, the home to NYU. I didn't need to say it; both of us obviously saw the irony of each of us going to the South Seas to meet up with a virtual neighbor. His smile told me he was amused by that too. His smile was luscious.

"I'm Austin," he said.

"Nathan here. What are you studying at NYU?"

"Theater arts. Dance mostly."

I would have guessed that. He carried himself like a dancer. It was one of the things that had arrested my view of him. He was different in so many things from other men I looked at . . . interacted with . . . let fuck me. I still couldn't quite figure out what the overwhelming attraction was. I could only acknowledge that I was drawn to him—sexually.

I continued the conversation. "And you needed to escape from that for a while—the dance?"

"The dance of life, I suppose," he answered. And then, when I looked at him quizzically. "I've had a relationship gone south."

"She left the dance?"

"He," he said, looking up at me and giving me a slight smile.

"Ah," was all I could think of answering to that. For some reason my heart was palpitating at double rhythm. "Ah," I repeated. "I guess I knew that. I saw you back on the beach in Suva. You went into the bushes with an old man. I wondered—"

"He had an exceptional cock. I just closed my eyes. I've found that older men, in general, have much better technique—and are more grateful to a young man who will submit to the fuck than other young men are."

"Ah, I see. For me, escape from the States was more a learning experience thing. I'm an international relations major. I wanted to hone up on my French. French is still one of the principle languages of diplomacy."

And I wanted to get away from the vanilla sex of my father's boyfriend, too, I thought—although he had stretching ways with toys that had put more exotic sexual testing in my mind. I hadn't come to the southern ocean just for the French. It was also for inventive, free-spirited, and bold Frenchmen, and for sexual testing and variety in experiences. And I hadn't been disappointed.

"And you are satisfied with what you found?" he asked. "With that writer fellow, Christophe? With the captain? I know you were in his cabin all night. I know what he was doing to you."

"You know that? How?"

55

"I know because if you hadn't been there, I probably would have been. That's likely where I'll be tonight—while you are being introduced to other members of the crew. I've been fucked nearly nonstop from New Caldonia to Fiji. And not just by the captain, but by the crew as well. You seem to have been taken up in that now too. Did you realize that was what you signed up for on this ship? Is that what you came to the South Seas for?"

"Yes, I'll have to admit, it is," I answered, looking directly into his face, not wanting that to be a show stopper for whatever he were moving into here—but not knowing what that could be. Austin obviously wasn't a power top; he may not even be agreeable to the position he'd been put in and that, evidently, thanks to Christophe and his story needs, I was experiencing as well.

"And it's not the same with you?" I dove in and asked. "You didn't come to the South Pacific to gain more and varied sexual experiences?"

There was a pause, but then he reached out and placed his hand on my forearm, and said, "Yes, I came here for that too."

I ached for him. But there was nothing I could think of doing for him. Two submissive bottoms, he evidently as attracted to me as I was to him. But out here on the isolated sea, at the mercy and the continued beck and call of power tops.

I thought he was about to say something, but we were both alerted to the bellowing of the first mate as he charged out on deck from the ship's superstructure, followed by other members of the crew.

"All hands on deck. Squall coming. Check the lashings on the tarps."

Both Austin and I scrambled up to do the first mate's bidding. As Austin probably already knew and, I understood, I soon was to find out, when the first mate called, you hupped to. And even then he could be very, very cruel.

* * * *

At least initially, I was glad for those strange raised boards all around my bunk. The squall had come and gone, but it had left the sea churning up enough that the tramp steamer was bobbing up and down and back and forth and it had been a real challenge to keeping our chow in our plates long enough to get it eaten at dinner—or in our stomachs afterward, for that matter.

Christophe and I spent the evening going over his collection of stories again, making sure that barebacking had been woven in where it would both foster arousal in the reader and be a natural element in the story.

"I will get a very nice return on these stories," Christophe said.

I noticed the "I"—that it wasn't a "we." It already seemed that I was the one covering our passage to Tahiti. What after that, though? I wondered. I was about to broach the subject when Christopher blindsided me.

"You going to fuck that young blond guy? I think his name is Austin."

"Excuse me? Me fuck him? You mean top him? I've never—"

"I watched the two of you together while the goods were being brought on board and again this afternoon—and he was the guy walking the surf back at the Suva resort who made your cock lurch, wasn't he? It's obvious you want to poke him. It's equally obvious he would like that himself."

"Obvious to who?" I asked. "Not to me." But now that someone had said it, yeah, I could see how it would be obvious that I wanted to fuck him. But I'd never topped. I was a submissive bottom. As far as I could see, so was Austin.

"Well, if you get around to it, I have some story ideas that would fit with it."

"Always the stories with you, isn't it, Christophe?" I exclaimed, rising from the chair in his cabin—a cabin that was far better appointed than mine was. It made me wonder again what he was doing to earn his passage—other than pimping me out, of course.

"The stories are giving you what you want—what you need," he retorted. "You could have left me in Suva. You didn't need me to carry you until the recovery of your funds came through. Surely you figured that out for yourself. You could have just walked along the surf line at the resort, like the guy you're pinning for, Austin, did the other day. You would have picked up a daddy almost immediately. Just like he did. He didn't get more than a hundred feet farther on the beach from where you saw him. That an old man was humping him in the bushes just up the beach while you were getting a double from those Brazilians. Young men like you and that Austin can stay on your feet just by lying on your backs and opening your legs. You stayed with me because of the stories—because you wanted what I could give you."

"I think that's enough of this for tonight," I said, as the ship lurched and I had to grab at the edge of a bureau. "Best place for me in this turbulence, I think, is in my bunk. And I need the sleep."

"On your back on a bed is always the best place for you, I think," Christophe said with a sneery smile. "And I wouldn't count on getting much sleep tonight."

I gave him an ugly stare.

"You know I'm right," he said, as I turned and did a zigzag approach to the hatch door out into the corridor.

He was right about the lack of sleep, of course. And I found out what the holes in the tall slats rimming my bunk were for. They were for the thick wooden rods that were slid through them.

I was nearly asleep when the men came into the cabin—filling the cabin to overflowing. All of them were naked or quickly getting there. I didn't have a chance—even if there had been a chance to be had. A couple of them held me down, my face pushed into the mattress, as I heard and felt the slide of the thick rods. They were been inserted in the holes in the side of the bed facing the room and rammed through corresponding holes on the other side. One rod down low, across the back of my neck, holding my head against the mattress. One further down, crossing under my armpits, forcing my arms up and over the side of the bed on one side and laying against the wall on the other, completely incapacitating them.

I was hauled up onto my knees and a rod pushed through just in the back of my knees, holding me in that position, my tail thrust up behind me. I had gone to bed nude, which made it convenient for them. I was completely and effectively entrapped now by the rods holding me in place, with my ass in perfect position for them.

I moaned and slobbered all over the mattress my face was pushed into as one of the crew members ate my ass out and prepared me for what then came—a succession of randy and muscular tramp steamer crew members mounting my ass and fucking me one after the other. Some wore condoms, but several barebacked me, and it wasn't long before I could hear as well as see their hard cocks sloshing around in the cum their mates had deposited inside me.

I could turn my head and see the snaking line leading from outside the open cabin door to the rear of the bed. They each were inside me more than once. And I could see that Christophe was in the room too—not only observing it all, obviously spinning another story for me to "inform" on the morrow, but also taking his turn in the fuck. I guess he wanted to be able to include the perspective of one of the gang bangers.

They were of different sizes and techniques and forcefulness. At the beginning I was counting just to have something to do while they were doing me, but I lost count. So I started visualizing the crew members in my mind, trying to deduce how many I had been fucked by and how many there were. Maybe they all weren't tops for men. But that was fruitless too—I soon saw that when a man pulled out of me, he just went to the back of the line to have another turn—and then another. This went on through most of the night.

I looked for the captain and the three mates, but, even though there was enough moonlight coming through the single porthole over the bed to discern one man from another in the line, I couldn't see any of those four. I was to subsequently find that we were on a five-night rotation during the fifteen-day sail between Fiji and Pago Pago. Captain Thorensen claimed me on one night, the crew got me on another, and a third night, one or more of the mates "entertained me." Two nights in the rotation were designated for rest, but Christophe usually claimed one or both of those for himself. Austin told me that he also was in the same rotation, so none of the crew members went long without sex with one or the other of us.

In the second rotation, I was imprisoned by rods on my back, a rod holding my throat down; one above my head, trapping my arms; and a couple under the small of my back, raising my pelvis. Then, the first time I noticed them, my legs were spread and raised and tied off on hocks in the cabin's ceiling by restraints. I had been pulled down to the foot of the bed, where I found the footboard collapsed down. The crew members just lined up between my spread legs and fucked me missionary style for hours on end.

In the third rotation, I wasn't bound. I was handed around for the crew members—all stronger than I could have resisted even if I tried—to take me in positions of their choice, either singly or in pairs—the pairs being either both an ass and a face fuck at the same time or a double penetration.

The mates were even rougher with me than the other crew members were. And, of course, there was Captain Thorensen and his specialties. As the days dragged on, some of the individual crew members were brave and forward enough to pick me off during the day, drag me somewhere, and have their way with me. The mates, though, did try to keep this to a minimum—

although sometimes they indulged themselves. For the most part, they only demanded blow jobs. It usually was all they had time for, and "getting it off" was what they focused on.

During it all, Christophe kept making observations, taking notes, and writing stories that did, in fact, make me melt at reading the reenactments and embellishments of what I was being used for onboard the *Pitcairn*.

One night I was in such a state of arousal after reading a gang bang sequence in one of his stories that I sat in front of the computer panting and pulling at my hard cock while Christophe embraced me from behind, ran his tongue up the side of my throat, and thrumbed my nubs with his thumbs.

"I do believe that the crew night visits to you are more satisfying to you than anything else you've experienced since you've been with me." When I didn't demur, he laughed and whispered, "You are such a slut for it." Then he pulled me over to his bed and fucked the stuffing out of me. I found I couldn't disagree with anything he said or did that night.

The men just evaporated after the first crew night. The rods were being pulled out of the bed slats, relieving the cramping I was beginning to feel. I sat up in the bed. The ship was stabile now, past the turbulence of the departed squall, but I had no idea how long the seas had been calmer. I looked up to see that all the men were gone—or nearly most of them. There was one man standing in the open door to the corridor.

"Austin?" I said. "Is that you?" Although I could only see him in shadow, I didn't know of any of the crew members who were that slender.

"Are you OK?" he asked, coming into the room. "I wasn't here. None of this was—"

"I didn't think you were here. But why are you here now? The captain. I thought—"

"He'd had a rough time with the squall earlier today. That pretty much wore him out. He's asleep. Hardly did anything to me. I thought you might need some attention."

"I got just about all the attention I could handle," I answered. I tried to smile. I was rubbing the back of my neck and the backs of my knees. The pain there rivaled that in my ass. I had no idea how many men had been inside me how many times. It was just more than I'd taken ever before. Far more. I could almost be grateful to Christophe and the captain for having opened me up so much with the fist fucking.

And, I didn't want to admit, it had me on a high. I'd taken them all. They had all wanted me, and I'd taken them all.

"I don't mean that kind of attention," Austin said. "I brought some lotion." He held up a bottle of it to prove he had it. "This stuff helps with me. If you'll lie on your back on the bed, I'll do what I can to take the sting away."

With a groan, I did so, and he came over, let the high side slat down—with me being surprised to learn that they all came down—and sat beside me on the bed.

"My muscles ache. What I really could use is a good body massage."

"I can handle that too," he said soothingly. He raised his other hand to show that he had a bottle of massage oil too. But that wasn't all he had in that hand. I saw the packets of condoms before he could tuck them between the mattress and the bedsprings.

"Hey, what the——?" I started to say.

"Shush," he whispered, putting a finger to my lips. "I promised I'll take good care of you. Turn over on your belly."

I did so, but my mind was racing. Had I guessed wrong? Was Austin versatile—a top as well as a bottom? Did I really want to be fucked again tonight, even if it was by Austin? Especially if it was by Austin. Although I was confused about what I wanted from him, I hadn't really thought that what I wanted was for him to fuck me.

But then he was dribbling the oil on my back and starting to massage my shoulder muscles, my arms, my back, and my thighs. I felt the other lotion, cool to the touch, streaming into my crack, and he was massaging me there too, gently rubbing the lotion over my buttocks and into the crack, massaging my rim. More lotion dribbled into the crack and down into my hole, and he was gently pushing it inside with a finger and gently massaging the first few inches of my channel.

With a moan, I raised my hips a bit, rising on my knees. If he mounted me now and fucked me, I'd gladly welcome him—even though I hadn't thought of him in these terms.

But he didn't. "Turn over," he said, his voice sounding shaky.

"I don't think I can." I answered.

"Because you're hard?"

"Yes, because I'm hard. Because there's nothing we can do about it."

"Of course there's something I can do about. Flip over."

I did so, and he wrapped a lotion-covered hand around my cock and begin stroking me slowly. I arched my back and moaned. His other hand massaged my chest and biceps, paying particular attention to my nubs. I could have sworn he was wearing shorts when he was standing in the door, but he was naked now, and in erection.

"You're going to jack me off?" I asked.

"More than that. I'm going to ride you."

"But . . . oh shit!"

He had taken my cock in his mouth and was deep-throating it. He took both my breath and anything I could say away, as I held his head between my hands and helped his mouth cavity rise and fall on the cock. The hand he wasn't massaging my chest with was busy cupping, separating, squeezing, and distending my balls, making me ache to shoot off.

Cock throbbing, needing to explode, I lay there moaning and murmuring, "But I don't . . . I can't . . . it's not what . . ." as he rolled a condom down my cock.

"Tonight you can and you will. I know you want me this way."

And then he was straddling my pelvis and lowering his ass on my cock. He felt tight and warm and I felt the muscles of his passage walls caressing my hard cock, undulating over the staff as he sank on me. I cried out and shot my load.

"Sorry. I said I couldn't . . ."

"But you proved you could. You did," Austin whispered, lowering his chest on mine. Our lips found each other and we kissed deeply. "We have the rest of the night," he whispered. "You can fuck me. You can be the top with me. I knew you could. Deep down, I think you knew it too."

And the surprising thing is that I found he was right. I never had considered that I could top a man. From the time my father's boyfriend initiated me, it had always been the man inside me. I had never considered I could top. But the funny feeling I'd had about Austin. It's because I'd wanted something different from him. I wanted to fuck him.

"But it was so fast," I murmured.

"The next time won't be," he answered, kissing my cheeks and my throat. Moving his lips down to my nubs.

The next time I thought, already feeling myself harden again just at the thought of it.

Austin laughed deep in his throat. "And the next time after that."

The next time came right away, with him rising back up on his knees and beginning to pump his passage on my cock again, riding me like a cowboy. This time I held out longer and he came up my belly before I ejaculated again.

I took charge the third time—coming after we had dozed and when the light of dawn was beginning to permeate the cabin through the porthole. He pulled the spent condom off me. I reached for another condom packet, but Austin grabbed my hand.

"No, not this time. I want it all from you. I want you to come inside me."

I rolled over on top of him, his belly to the bed. He raised his buttocks to me, and I fucked him hard and deep—fully in command—into the new day.

So, this was the way I found out I could top—and that I wanted to top Austin. In fact, my mind went back over the years since James had initiated me to sex and I realized that there had been others in my past that I had reacted to more from the role of a top than a bottom—I just hadn't known then what I wanted from them.

# Chapter Four: Pago Pago

"No shit? That's what you felt—or didn't feel?"

Christophe and I were sitting out on the portside deck, under the overhanging of the bridge above us, and working on the gang bang story.

"After about the fifth man, I plateaued out," I repeated. "Each successive dick didn't mean all that much—except perhaps for that Portuguese sailor. Every time he came around, I felt the stretch. And he had a distinct cork-screw type of working me."

"The Portuguese sailor. Alphonse. The younger, more muscular of the crew?"

"Yes, that's him. A thuggish-looking face that looks like he'd been hit by a two-by-four three times too many—but in the dark . . ."

"So, you wouldn't want to do that again? You have nothing that will enhance this story?"

I thought on that for a few minutes. I'd failed to say I didn't like it when he asked right after it happened. I still couldn't say that, on the whole, I didn't like it. "It was a mixed bag. I started to cramp after a while and was thinking more about that than about the men taking turns with me. But beyond the pain of being held in place by those rods, I sort of liked the feeling of being trapped like that—all decisions and responsibility out of my hands. No personal guilt for what was happening. And what was happening—that was arousing, I have to admit. The thought that that many men got hard for me. Repeatedly. That they came back for more. That they came. That I made them come."

"And did you come?"

"Yes."

"More than once?"

"Twice. Both time with the Portuguese sailor. He just had a way of going off beat when I was ready and triggering me." Blushing, I looked away from Christophe. I probably shouldn't have revealed to Christophe that the Portuguese sailor was special for me. Christophe picked up on everything—used it all to his advantage. And he later proved to do so in this instance as well. And beyond that, I didn't want to let him know of the three times later, with Austin—inside Austin. Who knows what Christophe would do with my awakening to the knowledge that I could top too—that there were young men, like Austin, who could make me want to top.

"Not for me? You didn't come for me last night. I was in the chain."

"I know you were. No, not last night. But I've come for you many times before. Last night, it was about the novelty of it—the shock, the imprisonment, the one cock after the other."

"So, there are emotions of the gang bang last night that you can give words to for this story after all?"

"Yes, I guess so."

"And after the gang bang. When Austin arrived. When you fucked him?"

Shit, I thought. "You saw that?"

"I see everything you do. I'm interested in everything you do. Not for this story, but—"

"Let's leave that alone," I said, angry and letting it show in my voice.

Christophe just smiled an enigmatic smile. "Do you want to fuck him again? Do you want the opportunity to do so?"

"Of course," I said, with a sigh, defeated by the man's persistence.

"I can arrange that. Come to my cabin after lunch. But for now, let's finish up this gang bang story. I trust you are satisfied that I have set it in that waterfront bar and the men taking you on a table, one of them pinning your throat to the table with a pool cue."

"Yes, that was fine," I said. But, in that one element, not as arousing as reality, I thought.

∗ ∗ ∗ ∗

I had Austin bent over the side of Christophe's bed, my hand cupping his throat, arching his back to me, capturing his mouth with mine as, the other hand on his hip, I pumped, pumped, pumped him deep and hard. I reached the hand around to find that his cock was hard now, a real handful when not flaccid. He moaned deeply for me at the pumping of both his ass and his cock.

He shot out on the bed and collapsed under me, as I heard the door to the corridor open.

"Fuck you, Christophe," I muttered, as I saw the Portuguese sailor move into the cabin, followed by Christophe, who closed the door and moved off to the side. "I know what you . . . oh, shit!"

The sailor came straight for me, losing his shorts, the only article of clothing he'd been wearing—on the way. He was in magnificent erection, no doubt having been prepped by Christophe already—by words or a blow job, I didn't know. And I didn't care.

And I didn't have a moment to think about it either.

He was at me, covering my back, grabbing my hips, forcing his cock inside me, beginning to pump me. I was still inside Austin, who was aware of the chain he was hooked up to, and who began to writhe and moan under me, his cock, still encased in one of my hands, coming to life again.

The Portuguese sailor fucked me at length, propelling my cock inside Austin's passage as much as his own cork-screwing, pistoning cock was working in my channel. Austin came first again, collapsing under me in exhaustion, murmuring his pleasure and sighing quietly. I came next, deep inside Austin, eliciting another deep moan from him. The Portuguese held out the longest, pulled out of me, and shot his load—a prodigious amount of it—across my lower back.

We weren't finished yet—and I had suspected we weren't as I'd already seen that Christophe had stripped down off to the side and was working his cock hard. When the sailor withdrew, Christophe took up his station, and Austin and I had to hold until he'd penetrated me, pumped, and fired his wad as well.

He patted me on the buttocks when he was done. "We'll leave you now to do whatever else with Austin you want to do. I'll go write up a story and you can go over it this evening."

Right. As usual, this was all for one of Christophe's stories. I no longer cared. Since Austin was here now, I took a few hours to do what Christophe said I could do—doing whatever else I wanted to do with Austin. It turned out he enjoyed some of the same positions I always had—from the same perspective he now was experiencing them.

\* \* \* \*

Austin and I had plenty of time between then and the ship's arrival in Pago Pago to satisfy each other—in addition to satisfying the rest of the crew. We also had time to make plans for Pago Pago that didn't necessarily meld with either Captain Thorensen's or Christophe's plans.

As far as Christophe was concerned, I couldn't figure out if he was losing interest or regrouping for something else he had planned for me. There were no new stories being written for more than a week. Christophe was using the time to polish and repolish the ones he had—all the time pressing me to unfold more emotions and sensations that would embellish them.

"You haven't come up with new ideas for several days," I said to him, both of us sitting in our customary deck chairs on the port side, one morning, only four days out of Pago Pago. "Are we coming to the end of this arrangement?" I didn't know whether I should tell him or not that I planned to try to split with him and the ship in American Samoan—that Austin and I were forming a pact.

"You're not getting enough attention?"

I shrugged. Let him think that's what it is, I thought. Better than him thinking I was working on wrapping this arrangement up.

"I have plenty of new ideas," he said. "Thinking back on an earlier conversation, I think East Europe might be a very creative destination. I have a publisher in Prague too who might like to print this collection."

"East Europe. You mean the vampire theme? Sucking and fucking to death?"

"One aspect, yes. Have you ever been bound, hung from a hook, tortured, and fucked?"

I looked sharply into his face. He was smiling, but it wasn't an "I am joking" smile. "The East Europeans do that?" I asked.

"They do it superbly. They could make you come continuously for hours."

"No, it doesn't really appeal to me." And, in fact, it didn't. I think I had gotten to the edge of fetishes that aroused me. I was, as I could, just moving between Austin and the Portuguese sailor. One on one, going both ways, was settling in to being enough for me.

"Ah, well. Think about it. I think the idea would grow on you."

"And how would we get to Prague?"

"Your finances should be in order well before when we reach Tahiti. I'm sure you could swing it all."

No doubt, I thought. And it came as no surprise that Christophe would suck at my teet as long as he could. He still hadn't suggested cutting me in on the royalties of the stories he was writing on my efforts on my back.

"Yes, it's something to think about," I answered as I rose from the deck chair. "Now I have—"

"Now you have to follow the Portuguese sailor who just signaled you," Christophe said.

"Yes, yes, I do," I answered, beyond asking for Christophe's permission to do anything—and beyond wondering how he managed to tune in to every sexual nuance going on around him.

* * * *

In the end, escape—or the simple parting of ways, I guess, as neither of us had really ever been a prisoner to what happened to us beyond the situation we were trapped in by the isolation of being on the vast sea—was fairly easy.

While we were helping to unload supplies for American Samoa at the Pago Pago waterfront and took on whatever Pago Pago could supply that would be wanted in Tahiti, where a major supply would be taken on for the more remote island along the northern tier of island archipelagoes, Austin simply broke away while I stayed to watch where the other crew members were. Neither of us was really engaged that much in the loading or unloading operations—or were expected to be. We were there for entertainment while the ship was on the high seas.

Austin simply went to the other side of the ship— the side facing away from the harbor—and manually let down one of the lifeboats. I joined him there, and we took the lifeboat around the headlands of the harbor and then walked back into town. We found the American Express office while the *Pitcairn*'s crew was still occupied with the exchange of cargo.

My line of credit had been reestablished. Austin confirmed his as well. And I learned something important about Austin. We went to a café well away from the waterfront and one that no crew member of the *Pitcairn* was ever likely to enter and drank some sort of coconut refresher and discussed where we would go from here—which increasingly looked to me like nowhere together. I wondered if it looked that way to Austin as well.

"So, I can get us both on a plane back to the States before we're even missed on the ship," I said, looking over the plane schedules I'd picked up at the American Express office and locating the airport on the southern coast of Tutuila, the main island of American Samoa. Pago Pago was on the northern coast, but you could just about see both the northern and southern coast when standing in the middle of the island here.

"Is that what you want to do?" Austin asked.

"Well, yes, of course. This is been about as much an adventure for me as I can take," I answered. But the way he fluttered his eyelashes at me made me reach out and stroke his forearm. "Not that I'd change having done it, of course," I added. "Especially meeting up with you."

Got that right, I thought. I don't know how long I could have gone without realizing that there were men I liked to fuck—that being fucked needn't be my whole sexual experience. In some ways, I went higher with my dick inside Austin than when I was being fucked by another man.

"I'm not sure I'm done," Austin said. "I may press on to Tahiti. Might even return to the *Pitcairn*."

"To be used like you were?"

"I like being used—even roughly. It's what I came to the South Pacific for."

"But why then—?"

"You were being used too hard," he said. "I wanted to help you get away. You seemed to want that too."

"But I thought the two of us . . . if this is about not having the plane fare home—"

"You never asked me my full name, Nathan. It's DuPont. I can pay my own way home."

"Oh," I said. If my family was considered rich in Philadelphia, the DuPonts were considered filthy rich all through the Mid-Atlantic states.

"Let's think more on this," Austin said. "I don't want to do anything hastily. I do care for you."

How much and in what way? I wondered. I also wondered how I really felt. In the euphoria of what I'd discovered about my sexuality and how Austin fit into that, I hadn't thought too hard about the implications.

"Let's go to a waterfront bar and get plastered," I said. "This coconut swill is nearly undrinkable."

"We can't go to the Pago Pago waterfront. *Pitcairn*'s crew will be crawling over that as soon as they are finished loading the ship."

"There's another waterfront—a rougher one, I'm told. There are hydrofoils going to Western Samoa almost hourly. We can be in Apia before dark."

And we were—and in a bar with much the same atmosphere as a series of stories in Christophe's collection. Sitting there, with Austin, while the rough life of sailors in an out-of-way port swirled around us, I had the slight regret that Christophe wasn't here to give me a chance to fold in the sights, sounds, and smells of the bar into the stories he'd written. If I'd ever come in contact with him again, I'd have to go over those stories with him again.

Both of us sat there at a table, observing and being observed. We must have been like a bonanza of two honey pots dropped into a congregation of bears. After the first drink, we didn't have to pay for another one. They kept coming from hulky sailors of all nationalities, who moved around us, maintaining a bead on us with their eyes, smiling little leery smiles, licking their lips, throwing air kisses when they established eye contact with us.

For my part, I found myself looking beyond the bruiser hulks to a young, dark-headed, almost effeminate young man sitting on a stool at the end of the bar. He was barely dressed in low-rise jeans and a half-cut T-shirt that showed a thin waist and a small silver ring in his belly button. I could tell he was French by the way he formed his words when talking with the bartender. But he was half something else too. Polynesian, probably.

What I noticed about him is that he kept looking at me and fluttering his long eyelashes. He was beyond cute. He was beautiful, his olive skin flawless. He was wearing sandals without socks and he had painted his toenails a fluorescent blue color—to match the color of the nails on his fingers. If he had done this to promote a man to think about sucking his toes, it had worked with me.

While meeting his gaze from time to time, I realized that he was waiting for me. He was being approached repeatedly by one sailor after another, but, while smiling at them, he obviously wasn't giving them what they wanted. I got the distinct impression that he was waiting for me to come for him.

"Austin," I said, turning toward him to see that he was flirting with his eyes with two muscular sailors who were leaning into each other at the bar but were drilling Austin with their eyes—obviously with another form of drilling in mind.

Austin broke eye contact with them and turned to me. He was smiling broadly, and I didn't get the impression the smile had just been plastered on for me. The realization hit me that there was nothing in terms of romance or a relationship either there or building between the two of us. Austin liked being fucked and had been attracted to me within this context. Little more than that. And I had perhaps thought I'd fallen for Austin more than I really had just because he had been the catalyst for my discovering that I wasn't just a bottom—that I was versatile.

"I agree, Nathan," he said, holding the smile and reading my thoughts. "It's been a real blast. Here, let me give you my contact information in the States. I'm sure I'll be back there at least for the start of school in August. I'll include my e-mail." He took a napkin and jotted his information. I took the opportunity to do the same, although he hadn't asked for it.

We slid the napkins across the table, our hands touching, but not lingering. It was over. I knew it and so did he.

"Gotta go take a piss now," he said, standing and heading for the back wall of the bar. The two muscular sailors at the bar followed him. I knew they would.

Still, I waited for a good fifteen minutes, my attention increasingly going to the young dark man at the end of the bar. His interest in me obviously increased as well.

A sailor started moving toward the table, and I rose, heading for the back, for where the john was, as much to avoid him as anything else. In the corridor, I didn't go into the john. My feet carried me farther down the hallway, to where I could see through a not-entirely closed doorway into a storage room, where the two sailors had Austin pinned down on his back on a low table. His head was hanging over one end, and one of the sailors was deep-throat face fucking him. The other sailor was at the other end of the table, holding Austin's legs spread and raised while, standing between his thighs, the sailor pumped his ass.

The noises Austin was making told me that he was thoroughly enjoying himself.

Back in the bar, the dark-headed honey was still perched on a stool, his eyes glued to the door into the hallway back to the john and to where Austin was getting what he obviously wanted. The young man's face lit up as I walked into the room and moved toward him. He inclined his head, and I nodded. He climbed down from the stool and headed toward the exit. I followed.

I fucked him in a small park not far from the bar, against a wall, his back against the bricks, his legs hooked on my hips, and our mouths plastered together as I thrust up inside him. He took me back then to a one-room flat above a restaurant, where a band played to a strong beat that I matched with the pumping action of a second and then a third fuck on his narrow bed—first missionary style and then doggie. Later in the night a side split.

The next day I took a plane out of Apia on a series of hops across the Southern Pacific—to Fiji and then Vanuatu, New Caledonia, and Sydney. No time or patience for tramp steaming now. I stopped along the way overnight, always picking up a small, yielding, almost effeminate young man at a gay bar and fucking the stuffing out of him on his own bed that night.

I never asked any of them their names—nor gave them mine. I'm sure I left them satisfied. I know I left each one of them fully satisfied myself—and exuberant that my sex life from here on out would be twice as interesting as before.

I kept the napkin with Austin's contact numbers on it, of course. One never knows.

I might even write a story about it someday. I'm sure my father's boyfriend would be happy to publish it.

# Chapter Five: Noah

I rolled back over and surveyed the body stretched out beside me. He was lying on his back, panting slightly, his legs still spread and knees bent. The pillow not yet out from underneath the small of his back. He gave me a wan smile, wrapped a hand around my neck, and drew me in for a kiss, barely giving me time to take the joint from my mouth that I had turned to take a drag from. We shared the smoke from the reefer in the kiss.

Such a cute little trick. I'd picked him up—or, rather, let him pick me up, since we were in his flat off Oxford Road now—at Sydney's Midnight Shift Club in the heart of the Australian city's extensive gay district. I'd gone to try out the bar there, only to find it was being renovated. I was waved upstairs to the club, where it was too early for their 4:00 p.m. opening, but where a bartender was checking over the inventory and was all "no problems" about pouring me a drink. The cute trick was perched on a stool at the other end of the bar. The bartender went to carry in some more liquor to even out his stock and the trick fluttered his eyelashes at me and asked if I might be interested in more than a drink.

I was, actually.

I could have taken him back to where I was staying—the City Crown Motel nearby, quite obviously a gay-friendly establishment—but in my air hops west across the South Pacific, where I had stopped in Fiji, Vanuatu, and New Caledonia, en route to Sydney to pick up a plane back to the States, I'd made a policy of going to the guy's room or a hotel room other than mine so I had the option of leaving when I wanted.

I was still reveling in the mere week's-old discovery that I was versatile. For two years I'd been in training as a bottom—in progressively more taxing fetish situations. I hadn't realized that I could enjoy going both ways until I was ridden on a tramp steamer en route to Pago Pago. I'd been exercising that knowledge back across the South Seas.

He was small—less than five and a half feet tall, I estimated—and with a willowy, dancer's body. In fact, I'd ascertained that he was a dancer—a pole dancer at the Midnight Shift. A strawberry blond. A classic "David" physique down to the pert cock and small, but distinctly separate balls. I had enjoyed rolling them about, distending them, and inhaling them into my mouth and sucking them in both cheeks. He had enjoyed that too. Just as he had tried the same with me and couldn't get them both in his mouth—and most certainly had gagging problems in deep-throating what I was packing. He'd been game, though. And experienced.

Slightly effeminate, as had been the others I'd practiced topping on my way back to civilization. And, although it was subtle, he used makeup to enhance his eyes and eyelashes and to produce unnaturally cherry-red lips. He'd also rouged his nubs, but I had sucked the makeup off them. And done his nails, in a lavender, very much like the sweet little thing I'd gone with in Western Samoa.

I don't really think the attraction was the type of men I was picking up to fuck. This was more of a transition, I believed—and hoped—and being sure if I could do the same with a more manly man. I certainly hoped I would be able to do so. As nice as I'd found pieces like this one to be for topping, there still was something missing in my sex life. But then there had been something missing in my life as a bottom too. Not arousal or lust, certainly—but something else.

I wondered if the makeup went with the slinky dresses I saw hanging around the small, one-room flat, or the high heels kicked into the closet. I'd never knowingly gone with a transvestite before . . . not that that mattered here because I knew this was a one-afternoon stand and he hadn't come on to me in that way.

I took another drag from the joint and shared it with him in a kiss, while my other hand glided down his smooth, boyish chest, the fingers dragging across the silver ring in his navel and his closely trimmed pubes as he shuddered when I grasped his cock and slow stroked him.

"Fuck me again," he murmured as we came out of the kiss.

"Liked that, did you?" I asked, still struggling over whether I could do this top thing convincingly.

"Loved it, stud. You're so big."

"Perhaps because you are so small."

"No, honey, I know hung and hard when I feel it. And you're still hard, and I want to feel it again."

"We could go for some supper and then come back."

"Can't sorry. Gotta go to work. You'll come and watch me dance?"

"Maybe. And afterward?"

"Fuck me again now. There may be no later. Can't come back here later. I have a roommate."

"A woman?" asked, gesturing to dresses hanging about.

"No, sweetie. Those are mine."

The flat was small—I could see it all from here. There was just this one double bed. "So you mean a boyfriend, not just a roommate?"

"He thinks so, and a big bruiser he is. That bartender who served you a drink at the Midnight Shift. Not as big where it counts as you are, though, honey. Com'on, mate, do me again. You do it so well."

What could I do? The pot was helping to keep me hard and aroused. I rolled back over on top of him, slid inside, and began to pump. He threw his arms around my neck, running fingers into the hair on the back of my head, arched his back, began to push down into every stroke, and cried out, "Oh, yes. Give it to me. Deep, hard. Oh, you stud! Ball me! Ball me hard!"

Later, after I'd left him and was walking down toward Circular Quay at the Rocks, one of the places where all Sydney mingled, to catch some dinner, I luxuriated in the thought that I'd obviously satisfied him as a top. That didn't mean I'd lost interest in bottoming as well, and maybe before I left Sydney on the flight out to Los Angeles the day after the next, I'd be able to get a little of that too.

I laughed at the realization that I'd neither asked the sweet little piece for his name nor given him mine. It had been the same way at all of the overnight bars on the hops by plane from Western Samoa to here. I wondered if sharing names was part of the "not quite" I felt in satisfaction in my sex life.

I don't know what had drawn me to Circular Quay and the view of the Sydney Opera house out on a small peninsula beyond, other than that I wanted to be in the middle of a lively crowd without direct interaction. I wasn't looking for a hookup. I'd had that today already. Tomorrow I planned some last-minute browsing in the area around Oxford Road, and the day after that I'd be on a plane for the States, my junior year summer exploration from Princeton over and ready to start my senior year in a month's time. And quite a summer it had been, traveling the South Pacific on tramp steamers supplying all of the small archipelagos across the sea. And quite an experience in sexual awakenings, just as I had hoped it would be.

I also don't know what drew me first to the busker leaning up against a closed ferry ticket window wall—his music or the clothes he was wearing. Or maybe it was the natural sensuality of the man. But, since I wasn't looking for sex, I'll pick the clothes he was wearing—and wearing quite well, I might add.

I had to laugh. Early in my summer adventure, I'd been seduced by a Frenchman—Etienne—who had coaxed me to take a tramp steamer with him from Nouméa, in the New Caldonia archipelago, to Suva, in Fiji. He had robbed and deserted me in Fiji. But he had taken not only my cash and credit cards but also my favorite fringed deer-skin cowboy vest and my cowboy boots. As melting as Etienne had been as a lover, missing those articles of clothing was what I remembered about him the most.

The busker was wearing them. Not my own vest and boots, of course. There were differences. But the similarities were close enough to arrest my attention and for me to make the connection. He was wearing a cowboy hat too, but as I hadn't lost one, I didn't focus on that. So, I stopped to admire the clothes, worn on top of tight, worn jeans, and a tight T-shirt, both tight because of his pronounced musculature. His face was easy to look at too. He was hirsute, but not grossly so. He maybe was in his late twenties, six or seven years older than I was. His faced showed both the cares and joys of a longer life than his body revealed him to be. Both the care and joy came through his rich baritone voice too.

He looked like the authentic rendering of an Australian cowboy, if Australia had them, and, with the country's vast outback, I realized they must have them. That, I guess, was what they called stockmen or jackaroos.

His songs were accompanied by a scruffy guitar with a sweet tone that matched his voice perfectly. I remained, loitering on the fringe of those passing by, for four songs. None of the tunes were familiar to me. All of them were good enough that I probably should have heard them before, though.

I eventually was embarrassed that I was hanging around so long when others were swirling around us, just passing by. All happy and boisterous. During the fourth song, I felt the isolation—not just of me, but of the busker too. But it wasn't an isolation of the two of us together, although I would have to say I found him arousing—not arousing in the sense of the new-found topping activity I was experiencing, but more in the older, more known sense of him on top of me, possessing me fully with his cock. I knew it would be a plump, long one. My trained eyes could see that in the basket of his worn, tight jeans.

The feeling of isolation in a bustling world—even from each other—saddened me. It didn't help that the song was a sad one too. I came closer to him. He looked up and smiled at me, a smile that went beyond the friendly. He interrupted the song long enough to give me the traditional "Gd-day, mate" greeting, revealing that he had noticed me stop and listen to him when all the rest had passed him by—even the ones who had dropped money in his open guitar case in passing.

I had only come closer to add my contribution to the case—a large sum since I was coming to the end of my visit and had Australian notes to burn. I mumbled something to him, he tipped his hat and started to say something, but I turned and walked away.

The music started again in my wake. He took up in the sad song where he had left off. I got the sense, though, that he was singing just to me now. There was a clutch in his voice. My instincts fought among themselves. Should I turn and return to him? Suggest a break and a coffee somewhere—and maybe a little fuck in the shadows? Or should I cut and run? Should I acknowledging that my "down under" across the Southern Pacific adventure ended the next day and just let it go?

I went directly back to the City Crown Motel, took a cold shower, and laid on the bed. I would forget him—but maybe tomorrow. In the meantime, I'd masturbate myself to sleep thinking of his body—wearing my cowboy vest and boots.

One of my dream scenarios was being out in the old, wild West in the States. Riding up into the Rockies on horseback with a hunky, horse-hung cowboy, and being fucked all night over a saddle and under the stars. It wasn't really a Brokeback Mountain dream—that movie had fallen far short of the sex action I wanted in my dreams. Having sex with a man was neither a frustration nor a guilty complex for me.

Tonight, it wasn't an American cowboy I dreamed of. It was an Australian jackaroo—I really liked that term for a hung man taking me. And it wasn't just any jackaroo. It was the busker from Circular Quay. My very own jackaroo, wearing only the fringed vest and cowboy boots I'd loved so well. He could wear his hat too, for all I cared.

\* \* \* \*

"Gd-day again there, mate."

The voice sounded familiar and when I looked around I confirmed I was facing the good-natured grin of the busker from the previous evening at the Circular Quay—the jackaroo of my dreams.

"Oh, hi," I said. "You're the singer from last night." He was even more than that, which was immediately electrifying me. We were both in a gay bookstore, the Bookshop Darlinghurst. The busker who had turned me on the previous evening was standing here in a gay book store—with a book in his hand. It had to be a gay book; it was a gay bookstore. So, he was probably gay. Extremely good information to know.

Everyone I'd told I'd be in Sydney had told me that I must visit the Bookshop Darlinghurst. It was my last day in Australia, and I had found, by walking around the Oxford Street area, that the bookstore was near my motel. So, here I was—and suddenly very glad I'd decided to visit here.

"Ah, an American accent. You an American then, mate? Just visiting Sydney?"

"Yes, American. And yes again, just visiting. I'm leaving for the States tomorrow."

"So, we'll have to work fast here." A grin of a smile.

I felt a chill go up my spine. I didn't know how to respond to that to not come off as easy as I was feeling in his presence. I wasn't about to say or do anything that would put him off me. He was really lighting my fire. So I didn't answer at all.

He pointed to the book I had in my hand. I'd barely opened it before he'd interrupted with his "Gd-day, mate," but it had made quite an impression on me—such a shock. A book this daring out on the table in a bookstore. I didn't know any bookstore in the States that wouldn't have a backroom for it, and, even then, probably locked in a cabinet and available only to customers who knew what they were looking for. It made me think of the stories the Frenchmen, Christophe, was writing as I traveled across the South Pacific with him. Stories meant for a small, highly jaded and well-heeled clientele.

I'd only had a moment to glance at some of the photographs—but what I'd seen was way beyond just provocative. More sensual even than photos of men fucking. More imagination and arousal food than that, which porn videos had taken the edge off of.

"I see you've found the Saxon book. Turn you on, does it?"

"I haven't had much time to look at it. What I've seen is shocking. It's—"

"The title pretty much reveals it, if you knew the photographer—Steven Saxon. The photos are all conquests of his. The title, *After Saxon*. You can see it. The fucker has the biggest dick I've ever seen. The photos are all taken after he's reamed them a new one."

"I got that," I said. "All of the poses."

"Showing their holes, making clear they'd been rebored larger than before they'd met Steve. So, does it turn you on?"

He had moved closer to me, an arm was around my back, the knuckle pressed into the table I was standing next to. He was significantly taller than I was, and it was like he was looking over my shoulder at the book, which I had open to facing pages showing two really good-looking guys, on their backs, obviously right after sex, their legs open, the men looking totally wasted, their assholes yawning open, their facile expressions leaving the impression of eyeballs swimming in rising cum.

"You call him by his first name and seem to confirm he's superhung. So, do you know him, this Saxon photographer?"

"Sure. We live in the same building. Artsy types live there. It's nearby. He's a visual artist. My gig is music. I compose."

"I thought maybe so," I said. "The songs I heard last night. Catchy, but I've never heard them before. Your own?"

"Yes. I sell them for others to record. But I try them out at Circular Quay to see how they do in public. Not so well last night. You were one of the few who stayed for any time—you were there for four songs. Left the biggest tip of the night. Wouldn't have forgotten you."

"Because of the tip? And you knew how many songs I'd stayed for?"

"I latched onto you the minute you showed up. Hoped you'd linger, and you did. You were the dream of my evening."

I blushed and looked back at the photos in the book. Should I tell him that he was the dream—the wet dream—of my night too? Was it my imagination, or was he leaning in closer to me?

"You interested in getting what these blokes got? I could introduce you to Steve. I'm sure he'd be interested in doing you and taking photos. You could be a model; could actually be a model, for all I know. Don't ask for an introduction unless you want to be lured into doing his will, though. He's a very persuasive man."

I shuddered, and I'm sure he was close enough into me to feel it. "I think he'd kill me."

"Never been doubled before? Never fisted?"

I didn't answer, so he assumed I had. And he was right.

"Not much different than that."

"You saying that from experience?" I asked.

"Page fourteen," he said, reaching over and turning the pages for me. "Did I tell you that Saxon was a very persuasive man?"

"Shit. That's you." I felt the deflation immediately. He was a bottom. He was gorgeous in the photo. Hung, still in erection in the photo; well muscled; melting hair patterns on his body. Even with that wide-open hole. The expression on his face reflected that he gotten excitedly what he wanted—and then some. No pay-for-gay expression there. I nearly laughed, though. All he was wearing in the photo was a fringed vest, cowboy boots, and a cowboy hat.

I was gaining experience as a top, but I hadn't reacted to him as a bottom. He was much too masculine and dominant looking. I'd only thought of getting something else from him. "So, you're a bottom." I doubt I was able to keep the disappointment out of my voice.

"Mate, if you'd go with me, I'd be anything you want. I do both. How about you?"

"Yes."

"Yes what?"

"I've done both."

"Going to buy that book? Want that introduction to Steve Saxon?"

"There's no way I could get this book through U.S. Customs. How about we go for a drink instead," I said.

"Sure. We could go to a bar. There are several nearby. Some of them even open."

"You said you live nearby. You have anything to drink there?"

"Yes."

"And you have a bed?"

"So, you want to fuck me or do you want me to fuck you?"

"Yes."

\* \* \* \*

It took us a while to get to the bed. We stopped and began stripping just inside the door of what was a very nice, well-appointed flat. The artwork seemed to be mainly Steve Saxon photos of sexy young men, but not like what he focused on in *After Saxon*.

He placed his hands on my shoulders and, taking the signal, I sank to my knees in front of him. He'd already pushed his shorts down to his ankles, and I took his cock in my mouth and gave suck. He appreciated that I could deep throat, even though he was built large. He wasn't cut and moaned deeply as I edged his foreskin with my teeth, pushed it back with my lips, and pressure sucked his bulb.

I had a slight indecision who would be doing the taking first, but he was anxious to get past the first fuck and pushed me down on the carpet near the door on all fours, mounted my hips, and pistoned me hard and deep. He took me in long thrusts, and as we both neared ejaculation, he laced his arms through mine in a full Nelson, pulling my shoulder blades up to his hairy chest, and latched onto one of my earlobes with his teeth as he thrust hard up into me again and again. I shot my wad off in a high arc across his living room floor and collapsed on the carpet as he withdrew, jerked the condom off his cock, and spread his load on the small of my back.

The second topping went to him as well, although we'd made to his bed. The first coupling being high heat, the second one was the one that made me never want to leave his bed. He made slow love to my body from my toes to my ears with his tongue and teeth, spending significant time at the halfway point, beyond which he refused to go until I'd ejaculated down his throat. Then he fucked me in a rocking motion, with us embracing as closely as we could, with me trapping his body to mine by locking my ankles behind the small of his back, our lips locked in a deep kiss until we came almost simultaneously.

And, although, with a muttered, "Now me, mate," he claimed his turn as a bottom, he remained dominant. I was trapped on my back under his greater weight and strength, and he rode my cock like a cowboy—like a jackaroo—not only rising and falling on my hard staff but also moving forward and back and from side to side as he rubbed every inch of his passage on my throbbing staff, massaged my pecs with his hands, and worked my nubs with his fingers and thumbs.

It was dark outside his windows before we were both satiated and exhausted. In the time I'd been with him, I realized what I had been missing in the two years of sex, including both bottom and top, classic positions and fetish, rough and not. It was passion. As arousing, heated, and fulfilling as the fucks had been before this, none were as passionate as I had with this beautiful Aussie. And it was the first time I thought of another man in terms of being a lover. Even though he'd remained dominant throughout, there had never before been the equal giving and taking—the concern for the pleasure of the other—that there was with this man.

"I'm afraid we haven't been introduced properly," he whispered after he'd rolled over on his side, taking me with him, still embedded inside him, and he nuzzled his way into my embrace. "I'm Noah."

"And I'm Nathan," I said. I'd come all the way back west across the South Seas, fucking young men almost nightly, and yet I hadn't told any of them my name. I was sure it was significant of something that I'd so readily told Noah mine—and that I had given him my real name. I knew he had. I'd taken a good look at the nameplate on his flat mailbox as we came up to his flat.

"You say you are flying out tomorrow?" he asked.

"I lied," I said. "I can stay for nearly a month longer." My mind was racing on the need to get to a telephone to cancel my plane reservations for the next day.

"If you don't want to stay wherever you're staying—"

"Thank you, I'd like that," I answered. "One thing, though, Noah."

"What?"

"Can you tell me where you got the fringed vest and cowboy boots you were wearing last night?"

"You only want me for my clothes?" he asked.

"Absolutely," I said, as I rolled him onto his belly, rolled with him, stretched out on his back, and started showing him he didn't have to be dominant every time.

~

95

# ABOUT THE AUTHOR

**Habu** is one of the pen names of a former supersonic spy jet pilot, intelligence agent, male model, movie actor, and diplomat. A wild youth in South East Asia was spent enjoying whatever sexual opportunities came his way, and much of his gay male writing is about recalling incidents from those days and inventing ones he'd perhaps have liked to experience. He now leads a very quiet and ordinary happily married family life.

An American, he is a published mainstream novelist and short story writer under another name and in another dimension of his life. He has written or cowritten (with Sabb) approaching 1,000 published short stories and over 100 published erotica e-books, primarily of gay fiction but also memoir, straight fiction and ménage fiction. His hand and creative writing can be seen in stories and books by habu, sr71plt, Dirk Hessian, Shabbu, and Stephen Kessel—among unrevealed others that might surprise readers. The fictionalized GM memoir *Flying High, Diving Deep* is loosely based on his life experiences. He can be found at the adults only gay male site www.BarbarianSpy.com, which he shares with Sabb and Dirk Hessian.

Our authors always like to receive feedback, and appreciate it when readers post reviews at distributors and other sites.

## BarbarianSpy
### FOR LITERARY HEAT

**Not all books listed below may currently be on release.**
\* indicates the book is available in paperback and e-book.

**BOOKS BY CHRIS CROSS**
**Multisexual Adult Romance**
Pulaski Square

**BOOKS BY ALEX LOCKHEED**
**Transgender Romance**
Meeting Jenna
**Transgender Other**
Being Sarah

**BOOKS BY DIRK HESSIAN**
**Xtreme Historical Erotica**
The King's Men
Shores of Tripoli
Prophecy of Noto
Pretender's Fate
**General Historical Erotic Romance**
To the Hessian Hills
Fire Down the Valley\*
Constantinople\*
The Beautiful Way\*
Blue and Gray
Colonel's Treasure
Beginning of Time
Labyrinth

# BOOKS BY HABU
## Gay Erotica
## Memoir Faction
Flying High, Diving Deep*
## Xtreme Erotica
Tramp Steaming*
Escape to Girne
Silas' Choice*
Last Call
Choke Hold
Apyko: The Greek Pimp
Visits of the Schlange
Second Coming: Emile La Cour Unleashed
Vortex: Sacrificed by Curiosity*
Dark Angel Sounding *(in e-book & included in Sounding:Ultimate Control Paperback)**
Sounding: Ultimate Control (*Print Only*)*
Sounding Five *(in e-book & included in Sounding:Ultimate Control paperback)**
## Romance
Rain Check
Built for Pleasure (Sci Fi)
Danny's Choice
Pull of the Groove
Sugar n Spice Christmas
Friday Nights with Lenny (Christmas Romance)
Snowy, Snowy Nights (Christmas Romance)
Tank n Bull
Sail to the Sun
War Letters
Ravens Roost
Caribbean Cruise Top to Bottom
Arena Stage
Trading Partners (Valentine's Day)
Four Coins
Lower Than the Heart (Valentine's Day)
Brambleton
Gotta Keep Trying

Finding Amnad
Platres Conclave
**Other Novels/Novellas**
Temptation's Clutches*
Descent into Chaos
Escape to Girne
Journey Through Abilene
Harmony and Dissonance
Stallion Station
Racing With the Devil (espionage suspense)
Cruising Gigolo (bisexual)
Prepared in Cape Verdi
Gilded Cage
House on Park*
Anything for Ambition
Dance of the Ravishers
Hard Knocks U*
My Neighbor's Spa*
Man's Man: Tales of a High Priced Gay Hooker*
Trip Money
The Indian Doctor
Sailorboy
Home to Fire Island
**Murder Mysteries**
Death on a Ping Pong Table
Clint Folsom Mysteries Compendium Volume 1*
Death to Blonds - Stolen Judgment (Clint Folsom
Mystery)*
Clint Folsom Mysteries Compendium Volume 2*
**Gay Erotica Anthologies**
Earth Cry*
Shunga
Habu's Christmas Balls
Eight in D*
DevilMENt
Silas' Choices*
Stallion Station (A Novella in Parts)
Eleven to the Dogs*

Fifty Seventy*
Spy Tails 001*
Spy Tails 002*
Doubled*
Doubled Again*
Tails in the Tropics*
Tails in the Med*
Tails in the West*
Rough Riders*
Grab Bag 1*
Grab Bag 2*
Grab Bag 3*
Grab Bag 4*
Grab Bag 5*
Grab Bag 6*
Grab Bag 7*
Beyond the Beaded Curtain*
Habu's Christmas Balls
The Sporting Life*
Fetish Galore!*
**Literary Gay Erotica**
Cairo Surrender*
The Handyman*
Homeward Bound
Journey to Mirage*
**Bi-Sexual/Menage Erotica**
**Bisexual/Menage/Multisexual Erotica**
Two Men, One Woman*
Every Which Way
Vanishing Laura
Summer of Denial
Death on a Ping Pong Table
Cruising Gigolo
13 Ways for Halloween
Luther*
The Indian Prince*
**MF Erotica**
Chocolate in Vanilla*

## BOOKS BY SABB
Driver Reliever
Hiring in Hollywood
The Legend of Holleystone Grange
Surprise Encounters*
She is He
Wrong Man
Loyal to his King
Barbarian Tales - Book One - Traveler's Tales*
Barbarian Tales - Book Two - Journeys Begin*
Barbarian Tales - Book Three - The Inheritance*
Barbarian Tales - Book Four - Road to Persepolis*

## BOOKS BY SHABBU
Velvet Interrogation
Finding Jason
Dirty Pool
Operation Black Jade
Cigars!*
Angel in the Barn
Gayly Complicated*
Despoiling David
The Tree of Idleness*
I Met a Man
Rough Road to Happiness

## BOOKS BY STEPHEN KESSEL
**Gay Romance**
The Forever Man
Two Chances

## BOOKS BY KIM BLACK
**Lesbian Romance**
Transfixed on Tammie (F/T lesbian)